Totally Bound Publishing books by Hannah Murray

Perfect Taboo

The Shame Game

Sharing His Submissive

Collections

Naughty or Nice?: Santa Daddy

Sun, Sea and…: Sun, Sea and Satisfaction Guaranteed

Perfect Taboo

SHARING HIS SUBMISSIVE

HANNAH MURRAY

Sharing His Submissive
ISBN # 978-1-83943-722-9
©Copyright Hannah Murray 2021
Cover Art by Louisa Maggio ©Copyright July 2021
Interior text design by Claire Siemaszkiewicz
Totally Bound Publishing

This is a work of fiction. All characters, places and events are from the author's imagination and should not be confused with fact. Any resemblance to persons, living or dead, events or places is purely coincidental.

All rights reserved. No part of this publication may be reproduced in any material form, whether by printing, photocopying, scanning or otherwise without the written permission of the publisher, Totally Bound Publishing.

Applications should be addressed in the first instance, in writing, to Totally Bound Publishing. Unauthorised or restricted acts in relation to this publication may result in civil proceedings and/or criminal prosecution.

The author and illustrator have asserted their respective rights under the Copyright Designs and Patents Acts 1988 (as amended) to be identified as the author of this book and illustrator of the artwork.

Published in 2021 by Totally Bound Publishing, United Kingdom.

No part of this book may be reproduced, scanned, or distributed in any printed or electronic form without permission. Please do not participate in or encourage piracy of copyrighted materials in violation of the authors' rights. Purchase only authorised copies.

Totally Bound Publishing is an imprint of Totally Entwined Group Limited.

If you purchased this book without a cover you should be aware that this book is stolen property. It was reported as "unsold and destroyed" to the publisher and neither the author nor the publisher has received any payment for this "stripped book".

SHARING HIS SUBMISSIVE

Dedication

For anyone who has ever had a fantasy, and the guts to make it a reality.
You're a fucking rock star.

Special thanks to fellow author K.J. Drake, whose input was invaluable to me when I was writing the nonbinary character in this book. They were amazing, and if I've made any missteps, it's through no fault of theirs.

Sharing is caring.
—*Sesame Street*, probably

Chapter One

Rebecca crumpled up the last bit of newspaper and tossed it into the box she was using as a makeshift recycling bin. "Last box, all empty."

"Nice job, love," Nick said, slipping his arm around her from behind. He kissed the back of her neck, his beard tickling her skin, then rested his chin on her shoulder. "Let's haul this out, then I'll order dinner."

She leaned into him and surveyed the unpacking debris that had taken over one side of the living room. "How about you haul it out, and *I'll* order dinner?"

"A traditional division of labor?" he mused. "Very Donna Reed of you."

"Donna would make dinner, not order in," she reminded him, and tried not to giggle when he gnawed playfully on her neck. "And anyway, I did most of the unpacking."

"Because you didn't trust me to put your stuff in the right places."

"True." She turned her head to smile at him. "But it still counts."

"Hmm." He narrowed his eyes, the bright crystalline blue darkening slightly. "I'll take out the recycling, but you have to eat dinner naked."

She forced a frown, even though her pulse began to pound in anticipation. "That's not one of the rules we agreed on."

His lips twitched in a smirk. "It's not a House Rule, it's a Now Rule."

"A *Now Rule*?" she parroted, and frowned harder to keep the smile off her face. "What is that, something you get to invoke anytime you want something not covered by the House Rules?"

"It's a spur of the moment negotiation for a specific situation. If you want me to haul all that away by myself, you have to eat dinner naked."

She eyed the broken-down boxes and wadded-up packing material that covered half the room. After a day of unpacking and arranging her belongings in his—now their—loft, she was ready to sit down and relax, and eating naked didn't sound like too big a price to pay to do it. But she wasn't going to tell him that. "Eating naked is dangerous. What if I drop hot food on myself?"

"Order sandwiches," he suggested.

She looked at him with a horror that wasn't entirely feigned. "Have you ever had breadcrumbs in your crotch?"

"I can honestly say I have not." He arched an eyebrow. "Have you?"

"Well, no," she admitted. "But I've had sand in there, and I'm guessing crumbs would be just as bad. I want a napkin for my lap."

"For a napkin, you'll have to wear a butt plug."

I'll need a napkin for under me, too, she thought. Her pussy was wet just thinking about him plugging her ass. She sighed heavily, the picture of a beleaguered, long-suffering submissive. "Fine."

"Fine," he echoed, and bent to capture her lips. The kiss was quick, with a just a teasing hint of tongue. When he lifted his head again, his gaze was bright with amusement. "You're not fooling anyone, you know."

She forced her eyes wide and blinked, projecting innocence for all she was worth. "I don't know what you're talking about."

"Uh-huh." He slid his hand from her waist to her breast, where her nipple was trying to poke through her T-shirt. He gave it a firm tug, sending a quick bolt of sensation straight to her pussy. "You're sure that's the story you want to go with?"

"Give me a minute to think of a new one," she managed, and he laughed.

"Order dinner, then take a shower," he said, his hand light on her breast. She wanted to lean into him for firmer contact, but that would give him the advantage. Not that he didn't already have it, but still. "When you come back, bring the blue butt plug and the alligator clamps."

She was nodding before she caught the last part. "Wait. You didn't say anything about clamps."

"That was before you tried to fool me," he said, and squeezed her nipple hard enough to make her squeak. His grin was pure perverted delight. "Infractions require corrections, baby girl."

"I don't think that's fair," she said, breathless from the spike of pleasure-pain.

"Want to make it a butt plug, alligator clamps, *and* a vibrating egg?" he asked, his fingers still tight on her nipple.

Shit. She shook her head.

"Then say, 'yes, Daddy'," he advised, his eyes gleaming, "and do what you're told."

"Yes, Daddy," she parroted, and bit her lip when he released her nipple. She couldn't decide if she was relieved or disappointed, and gave him her best pout.

It just made him grin. "Good girl," he said, and kissed her one more time before striding to the pile of boxes.

Rebecca shook her head and walked around the free-standing wall that served to separate their sleeping space from the rest of the loft, her body humming with arousal. It was amazing what that man could do to her with those two magic words. Sometimes she wondered if he could *good girl* her to orgasm, using nothing but his voice and the approval she craved to get her there. She didn't think it was possible, but she wouldn't bet against Nick, or the powerful, incendiary effect he had on her.

It might have been embarrassing if she didn't like it so much. But she did, and so did he, and knowing that made everything okay. Besides, she had the same effect on him—he was just better at controlling his responses. Hell, he was better at controlling everything... including her.

She wondered just how he was planning to control her tonight, and pulled out her phone to order dinner.

With the sandwiches on their way—estimated delivery time, twenty-two minutes—she stripped out of her moving-day clothes of yoga pants and a T-shirt and headed into the bathroom. There were a lot of things to love about the loft—the high ceilings, spacious rooms with plenty of natural light, and secure, covered parking were all great—but her very favorite thing was the bathroom.

It was the size of the bedroom in her old apartment, and almost embarrassingly luxurious. There was a soaking tub long enough to fit Nick's lanky form with room left over for her, or she could just swim laps in it by herself. Two sinks on opposite sides of the room meant she didn't have to share counter or cabinet space, and while it didn't have a place for her to sit and do her makeup, she liked to do that in natural light, anyway.

There was a shower with rainfall showerheads in the ceiling that she could turn off with a touch of the state-of-the-art instrument panel when she didn't want to get her hair wet, and more shower heads set into the marble-tiled wall. There was even a bench, wide and deep enough to seat two people side by side—or two people with one on the other's lap—and massage jets set in the wall behind it.

The matching tile covering the bathroom floor was heated, the lights under the cabinet edges were motion activated so she never stumbled in the dark, and, best of all, the toilet was in its own separate frosted-glass-enclosed room. Not that she was particularly embarrassed by bodily functions, but sometimes a body needed to sit for a spell.

And on those occasions, it was really nice to be able to close the door.

She handled those bodily functions first, then stepped into the shower and tapped the wall panel to activate the rain showerheads. Moving day had left her feeling grimy, and even though it still felt like winter outside, she'd worked up a sweat. She might have lingered in the shower, letting the jets and hot water wash away the dirt and soothe sore muscles, but her stomach felt like it was trying to eat itself. Lunch had been several hours of physical labor earlier, and she was hungry.

She cleaned up quickly, washing her hair and scrubbing the sweat from her skin, then grabbed a fluffy towel to dry off. She wrapped it around her hair to soak up the excess water and keep it out of her way while she slathered on moisturizer, then hung it over the heated towel rack and dragged a comb though her dark locks. Her hair was getting to the long-enough-to-be-annoying stage, and she made a mental note to schedule a trim. She'd taken Monday off, assuming she'd be tired from a weekend of moving and organizing, so maybe she'd see if her stylist could squeeze her in.

She left her hair down to air dry and pulled on her robe. A moving-in present from Nick, the thick cashmere was soft, warm, and killer, fuck-me red. He'd said it had caught his eye because it was the exact color of her favorite lipstick, the one she always wore when she wanted an extra boost of confidence. She'd worn the lip color a lot in the three years she'd worked for Nick, and apparently, he'd become somewhat obsessed with it.

She didn't work for him anymore, and she rarely needed a boost of confidence these days, but she still wore the lipstick. It had a delightfully predictable effect on her lover, one that usually ended in multiple orgasms for her.

She debated putting some on now, but decided it was too much trouble. She left the bathroom and crossed the bedroom to Nick's side of the bed. He kept the toys they used most frequently in his nightstand, the butt plug and nipple clamps she sought sharing space with leather cuffs, dildos and butt plugs in a variety of sizes, a rechargeable wand vibrator and a leather paddle.

There were other toys in the hope chest at the foot of the bed, just transported from her old apartment that morning, and in Nick's fully stocked toy bag in the walk-in closet if he wanted a more involved scene. But he liked to improvise, so he kept the basics close at hand.

She tucked the plug and clamps into the pocket of her robe, then shoved a small bottle of lube into the other. He hadn't asked for it, but maybe she could score some points by anticipating his wants.

She'd take all the good-girl points she could get.

She walked into the living room just as Nick was opening the door to the food delivery, and the open floor plan of the space meant that both Nick and the young man in the open doorway saw her. She kept her hands in the pockets of her robe, fighting the urge to draw it more tightly around her. The fact that it covered her from neck to toes didn't make her feel any less exposed, and the objects she carried only added to the feeling. Nick knew, of course. It was in the gleam in his pretty blue eyes, in the quirk of his lips as he smiled at her. And, being Nick, he took advantage.

"Hey, baby," he purred, reaching out a hand in a silent order to come to him. She obeyed it without hesitation, her pulse pounding in her throat. "You remember Adam?"

"Sure," she said with an easy smile, her fingers tight on Nick's. "How are you?"

"Good, thanks," Adam said, his throat bobbing as his cheeks flushed. He was young, in his early twenties, working as a driver for several food delivery services to help meet his college expenses. Their neighborhood was his territory—if they ordered food, there was at least a fifty percent chance that Adam would deliver it.

He had a small, harmless crush on her, which Nick found amusing. Rebecca found it sweet...and when she was wearing a bathrobe with sex toys in the pockets, awkward.

She squeezed Nick's fingers again in silent admonishment before reaching for the bag Adam held. "Thanks for coming so fast. I'm starving."

"I had them throw in an extra pickle, just for you."

"Thanks." She smiled at him, holding the bag to her chest. "I love pickles."

"I know," he said, and flushed tomato red.

She cut her eyes to Nick, who winked back and pulled a couple of bills out of his pocket. "Thanks for the speed, Adam."

Adam took the tip, his eyes widening a little at the amount. "Hey, thanks, Mr. Saint, Ms. McBride."

"See you next time, Adam," Rebecca said with a little wave as Nick closed the door. As soon as it was shut, she shook her head at Nick. "You're terrible."

Nick merely grinned. "Seeing you in that red robe probably made his day. If you'd come out naked, he'd have passed out."

She rolled her eyes and headed for the kitchen. "Good thing I'm not going to do that, then, isn't it?"

He took the bag from her and unpacked it, setting the sandwiches, chips, and pickles—two for her, one for him—on the plates she laid out. "And if I told you to?"

She pulled a couple of bottles of beer out of the fridge and met his raised eyebrow with one of her own. "Involving other people in a scene who have not explicitly consented to being involved in said scene falls under the heading of Things I Will Use My Safeword For."

"God, I love it when you get prissy." He grinned and smacked her ass. "Reminds me of all those times I wanted to bend you over my desk and fuck the sass right out of you."

She resisted the urge to rub her stinging butt and scooped up her plate. They didn't have a dining room table yet, because Nick had never seen the need and her old place hadn't had room. They were going to go shopping for one together, but in the meantime, their dining options were the living room or the breakfast bar. "Where do you want to eat?"

"Living room," he decided, and followed her over.

She was lowering herself to the sofa when he said, "Don't sit."

She glanced down, thinking she might have been about to sit on the television remote, but there was nothing there. "Why?"

"Because." He set his own food on the coffee table, grabbed one of the pillows from the corner of the sectional, and tossed it on the floor at her feet.

Her belly fluttered as she contemplated the cushion on the floor. "This is new."

Chapter Two

"Any objections?" he asked, and she glanced up at him.

He was watching her carefully, a slight frown furrowing his brow. She was used to Nick frowning—when she'd worked as his assistant, it had been his default expression. He laughed more readily now, and sometimes she caught him smiling at her for no apparent reason, but the frown still popped out when he was thinking or concentrating.

"No objections," she said faintly, the fluttering in her belly picking up speed. Frowny Nick turned her on. "I'm just wondering why."

"We're still figuring out our D/s dynamic," he explained. "I want to see how this feels for us."

It feels…not bad, she thought. *A little strange, a little uncomfortable, but not bad.* "Okay."

"But first things first," he said, and dipped his hands into the pockets of her robe.

She stood still, though the brush of his hands against her body through the cashmere made her want to wiggle. He plucked the lube from one pocket, the plug and clamps from the other, and raised that eyebrow again. "Lose the robe."

She slid it off and let it fall, bracing herself against the chill in the air. They were still negotiating the ideal thermostat setting, and it was a little too cool for her comfort. But while the air might have been chilly, his gaze was warm with appreciation as he took in her nude form.

Liquid heat pooled in her belly, and her pussy grew damp with arousal. Well, damper—she'd been turned on since he'd said the word "butt plug." Her nipples, soft from her shower, reacted to both the chill and her arousal by bunching up tight.

Nick dropped the lube and plug to the coffee table and held up the clamps. "Nipples first, then," he said, and stepped forward. "Behind your back, love. Hands to elbows."

She reached behind her, folding her arms against her back so she grasped the opposite elbow in each hand. The pose forced her shoulders back and her breasts forward, and he smiled with approval.

"Love your tits," he murmured, and bent his head to run his tongue around her right nipple. Her breath caught in her throat at the sweet sensation, then moaned as sweet went sharp when he took her into his mouth to suck.

He worked her nipple for long moments while she struggled to maintain her pose. She wanted to grab his head and hold it tight to her breast, to encourage him to take more, go harder. When he raised his head, she swayed toward him, her body instinctively seeking his touch.

"Stay still," he said absently, his attention on her breast. Her nipple was a dark ruddy brown, wet from his mouth and throbbing lightly with the beat of her heart. He cupped her breast in one big hand to hold it still, and she let out her breath in a long, slow exhale as he applied the clamp.

Pain bloomed almost sweetly, the slow exhalation helping mitigate the worst of it, and after a moment the sharp pinch faded into a dull throb that echoed deliciously in her pussy.

"A little more, I think," he said, and turned the screw to tighten the clamp, his careful gaze on her face.

The pain brought tears to her eyes, his low voice coming to her through the roaring in her ears. "Easy, sweetheart. Breathe in and out."

She obeyed, her watery eyes on his, and after a moment she relaxed, her muscles easing as she surrendered to the pain.

"That's my good girl," he said, his voice ringing with pride and approval, and bent his head to her other breast.

When both her breasts were clamped and throbbing, he picked up the plug and the lube. "Turn around, bend over, and put your hands on the floor."

She immediately moved to obey, though she did it carefully. Keeping her breasts from swaying was impossible, especially since they were unsupported, but moving without bouncing helped keep the pain in her clamped nipples at a manageable level.

Which was no doubt why he popped her on the ass and made her jump. "While we're young, please."

She didn't bother even trying to hold back her choked gasp at the pain that radiated from her nipples outward as her breasts swayed heavily. If the last few months had taught her anything, it was that trying to keep things from Nick never, ever went the way she wanted it to. He always knew, and unless he'd ordered her to stay quiet for some reason—like to minimize their chances of being caught, or just to torture her—he didn't want her holding back.

He wanted every squeak, moan, squeal and scream. And if she was begging, oh, he wanted that too.

She suspected that *please, Daddy, please!* was his second favorite phrase in the whole world, second only to *I love you, Daddy.* Sometimes if she said the second, she wouldn't have to say the first, but only until next time.

So when she finally completed her turn and bent at the waist to plant her hands flat on the floor and her breasts slapped against her thighs, igniting the fire in her nipples again, her whimper was both audible and pleading.

"Very nice," he said with a chuckle, clearly not in the mood to be merciful. "Have I mentioned how much I love your flexibility?"

Damn yoga. She sucked in a breath to thank him—*thank you, Daddy* also ranked pretty high on his list of favorite things to hear—but the words died when the plug, cold and wet with lube, pressed against her asshole.

The plug was Nick's favorite, and she called it the little blue devil. It was innocuous enough looking—small in size, it was designed with a long, narrow base that fit more easily between her cheeks than one with a round base, making it comfortable for long wear. But its unusual egg shape meant she felt much fuller than she did with most other plugs, and the lack of a tapered tip also meant that inserting it felt much like it did when Nick forced the broad, blunt head of his cock into her asshole.

And when he did it with no previous stretching, like he was doing now, it felt like a Mack truck plowing her open.

"Breathe, love," he reminded her, increasing the pressure, and she concentrated on sucking in air and pushing it back out as her asshole stretched and burned and finally gave way, the fat silicone egg spreading the narrow channel wide. Then her sphincter closed down on the narrow neck of the plug and the long slim base was sucked firmly between her cheeks.

She stayed there for a moment, panting through the discomfort. But while the burn and the stretch on her asshole faded, the sense of fullness remained, and her pussy throbbed in response.

"*Very* nice," Nick murmured behind her, and she nearly jumped again when he skimmed a firm finger along her pussy. He circled her clit without touching it, teasing and light. Her legs flexed without conscious direction from her brain, pushing into his touch, and he chuckled.

"Greedy girl," he said, and his hand dropped away. "Stand up."

She straightened, shivering as the plug shifted inside her and her breasts swayed. The pain in her nipples distracted her from the fullness of her ass and vice versa, scattering her focus.

Nick's hands closed on her shoulders and turned her to face him, moving her much faster than she would on her own, and her moan this time was one of pure arousal.

He looked down at her, his bright blue eyes full of love and mischief and nefarious intent. He skimmed a finger down her face, tracing the heat she knew had turned her cheeks pink, and his mouth curved. "Rebecca."

"Daddy," she breathed. He was looking at her as though he wanted to either cuddle her in his lap or strap her down and torture her, and not knowing which was coming turned her on almost as much as the clamps and plug.

"Greedy," he repeated, knowing exactly what she was asking for. He leaned down and kissed her, the soft brush of his lips nowhere near the hard, bruising contact she craved, and raised his head when she rose on her toes to take it deeper. "No."

"Daddy," she said again, whining this time.

The smile dropped off his face, one eyebrow going up as his eyes narrowed, and she was suddenly shivering for an entirely different reason. "If you make me say no one more time, you won't like the consequences."

She dropped back down, trying not to pout. There was a fine line between begging and topping from the bottom, and she knew from experience that crossing it wouldn't end well. "Sorry, Daddy."

"There's my good girl." He kissed her again before stepping back. "Sit down and eat your dinner."

Sighing, because he was apparently determined to feed her before he fucked her, she lowered herself gingerly to the pillow. Her robe had fallen over it, providing a barrier for her wet pussy, and she was grateful. She'd still have to hand wash the robe, but she'd rather do that than have to send the cushion out to be dry cleaned.

She settled cross-legged, holding her breath as the plug shifted inside her and her breasts swayed, shooting pain through her nipples. When the stars faded from her vision, she leaned forward to grab her plate off the coffee table, and set off another round.

"How're you doing, sweetheart?" Nick asked, and Rebecca turned to find him sitting in his chair, watching her with a smirk.

"Fine," she lied, and tried not to squirm. She was so damn horny she could barely think, and wondered if she could convince him to fuck first, then eat. "You know, I'm really not that hungry," she began, and right on cue, her stomach rumbled.

"Lying will be severely punished," he warned her, and picked up his sandwich.

She scowled at her stomach. "Traitor," she muttered, then set her plate in her lap and picked up a pickle.

They ate in silence for a moment, both of them ravenous after the long day of unpacking and organizing. Rebecca's attention was divided between her full ass, her compressed nipples, and the odd little zing that had crackled through her when Nick had suggested opening the door to Adam with her naked.

"What are you thinking about?"

She held up a hand, pointing at her full mouth. She swallowed, then said, "That thing at the door."

"What thing at the door?"

"Would you really ask me to come out naked when Adam was here?"

He crunched into his pickle. "No. For two reasons."

Rebecca brushed crumbs from her legs. Dammit, she'd forgotten to get a napkin, and after she'd taken the butt plug for it, too. "Which are?"

"The first is the same reason you gave—Adam's not a party to our kink, and we're not going to make him one without his permission."

She'd been pretty sure he agreed with her on that, but it was nice to hear him say it. "And two?"

"I don't trust him."

She blinked. "You have to trust him for him to see me naked?"

"Not as much as I'd need to trust him if he was going to actually play with us, but at least enough to know he wouldn't tell everyone that part of his tip is tits and ass."

She almost choked on her pickle. "You'd invite him to play with us?"

"No."

She sagged in relief as the tension left her body.

"I just said I don't trust him enough for that."

And the tension was back. "What if you did trust him?"

His grin was wolfish. "Then that's a whole different ballgame, isn't it?"

"You're saying you'd let another man—"

"Dom," he corrected, and arched one brow when she gaped at him. "Which is partly why Adam's not on the list."

Her eyes bugged out. "There's a *list?*"

"Not a written one," he said, eyes dancing with humor. "It's more of a mental list."

"Why is there any kind of list?" she wanted to know.

"Because you want it," he said simply.

Shock kept her silent for a full five seconds. When she finally found her voice, it was little more than a squeak. "I do not."

"Liar," he said softly.

"I'm not lying," she protested, ignoring the shiver that ran through her at the tone of his voice.

"No?" He set his plate aside and leaned forward, looming over her. "You think I'm not paying attention whenever we role play double penetration? You think I don't see how wet and wild you get when we pretend I'm going to offer you up to my friends?"

"That's different."

"How?" he asked.

"I'm monogamous," she began haltingly, hoping to do an end run around the question.

"As am I," he said calmly, then paused. "Well. Monogamish."

"What does *that* mean?"

"It means that while I have no desire to be polyamorous, or have other partners on a regular basis, I also don't mind sharing on occasion. And the idea of me sharing you makes you hot."

"I… That's just a fantasy."

"It can be," he agreed calmly. "If you want it that way."

She swallowed, her thoughts a muddle as she stared at his face. It was true, she liked the idea of him passing her around to his friends for their use, a toy to be enjoyed. But she'd honestly never thought about making it a reality. Was that what he wanted?

"Do you want to share me?" she asked, forcing the words out.

"Yes," he said baldly, the predatory gleam in his eye at odds with his relaxed posture. "I do."

"Why?"

"Because you'd love it," he said softly. "Daddy's little slut. That's what you are, aren't you?"

Her breath hitched, heat flooding through her as she stared at him. "Yes."

"Say it."

Arousal pulsed through her, low and heavy like the base line of a song. "I'm Daddy's little slut."

He leaned forward to loom over her, close enough she could see the cords in his neck straining. "You wouldn't lie to Daddy, would you, baby girl?"

"No, Daddy," she whispered, fear and need twining together in her gut, confusing her.

"No, you wouldn't." His smile was soft, with a hint of menace that made her pulse pound faster. "So when I ask you how wet your pussy is right now at the idea of me sharing you with another Dom, you'll tell me the truth. Won't you?"

Oh, God. "Yes, Daddy."

He was silent for a moment, drawing out the torment. Then, "How wet are you?"

She licked her lips, unable to look away from that penetrating gaze. "I'm going to have to wash my robe."

He chuckled, rich and deep, and sat back in his chair. "I bet. Stand up."

Chapter Three

She pushed to her feet, using the coffee table as leverage, locking her knees against the shaking in her legs. She took the two steps that brought her to him, her shins bumping into the edge of his chair.

He ran his hands down the backs of her thighs. "Flex your knees," he murmured, stroking the sensitive skin with his thumbs. "I have plans that don't include you passing out. How are these doing?"

Sitting in the chair, his face was nearly level with the chain that connected the clamps—if he leaned forward an inch, he'd be able to take it in his teeth. "They're fine."

He shook his head with a soft tsk. "I'll have to fix that. Hold still."

He reached up, steadying her breast with one hand while he grasped the clamp with the other, his eyes locked on hers as he tightened it. It was such a small difference, barely half a turn of the screw, but the pain that screamed through her already tortured flesh was so intense that her knees nearly buckled.

"Hold on to me, Rebecca," he ordered, and she latched on to his shoulders, staring down into the crystalline pools of his eyes as she breathed through the pain. "Good girl. Keep breathing."

He reached for her other breast, waited for her to inhale, then timed the tightening of the clamp with her slow, controlled exhale. Despite the breathing trick, the pain stabbed into her, exquisitely sharp, before fading into a deep throb that seemed to travel from breast to loin and settle there, heavy and hot. Her pussy clenched, achingly empty, which made her anus clench, achingly full.

It was confusing and painful and so goddamn hot she nearly came right there.

"Not yet," he warned, and she gritted her teeth against the pleasure. He'd begun denying her permission to come recently, making her wonder if he wasn't more of a sadist than a Daddy. Or maybe a Daddy sadist. God help her.

"Good girl," he praised, and pressed a gentle kiss to her sternum. "Now, where were we?"

She wasn't about to tell him, but then, he didn't need her to.

"Oh, right. We were talking about how the idea of two Doms makes you wet," he went on. "Doesn't it?"

"Yes, Daddy," she sighed, helpless to do anything but answer honestly. It was an exciting fantasy, two men at once, and one of her favorites. It was what she went to most often when masturbating, or when she wanted to get off fast. But she'd never really thought to make it a reality.

Until now. Until Nick.

"Of course it does," he murmured, pulling her attention back to him. He palmed her ass with one hand, digging his fingers in while he toyed with her pubic hair with the other. She'd just had a wax, which meant that everything was bare but for the small patch at the top of her mound that she left wild and untrimmed. He tangled his fingers in it, tugging gently upward so the skin around her clit moved, an indirect caress that he knew would only drive her higher. "The only question is, how wet?"

She opened her mouth to answer, but she needn't have bothered. He moved his fingers lower, sliding past her clit to the slick, swollen folds below. His soft laugh was filled with triumph, and she automatically spread her legs in response.

"Such a good girl," he praised, his soft touch at odds with the hard glitter in his eyes. He looked almost wildly aroused, his jaw and his breathing harsh, and the muscles in his shoulders were tight under her hands. But he kept his touch light and teasing, one finger circling her slippery hole so gently that she wanted to scream.

He dipped his finger inside, barely breaching the opening. Her pussy flexed, the muscles clenching down in an attempt to suck the invader in as her hips rolled to get closer. All she got for her efforts were a low chuckle and a slap on her ass, which made the plug inside her shift, which made her even wetter.

"Such a greedy slut," he crooned, his tone turning what could have been admonishment into praise. His hand dropped away from her pussy, eliciting a whine of protest from her that he ignored. He slapped her thigh, the wetness of his fingers adding a stinging bite. "Spread."

She tightened her hands on his shoulders for balance and inched her feet farther apart, stopping only when her legs bumped into his splayed knees.

"Hmm." He frowned, eying the space between her thighs. "Not wide enough. Climb on."

It took her a moment to understand that he wanted her to sit on his lap. Using her grip on his shoulders for balance, she lifted her knees over his, but his legs were so far apart she had no support. "I need your knees closer together."

"I don't think so," he said, a feral glint in his eyes. "I think this is just right."

She was spread so far out the only thing holding her up was her grip on his shoulders. She tightened her core and her legs, muscles quivering as she fought to keep herself from falling.

"Hands behind your back."

She shook her head, her still damp hair sliding over her skin. "I'll fall."

"You won't."

"I'm not strong enough—"

"Do you trust me?"

She stared at him, losing herself in his eyes. "Yes."

"Then put your hands behind your back," he repeated, and she did.

She wobbled slightly and let out a squeak, panic overwhelming the pain that burst in her nipples as her breasts swayed. His hand tightened on her ass, steadying her. "Put your hands on my knees, use them to keep your balance. But if you feel like you're going to fall, let me know."

She nodded, shifting her hands behind her to grab his legs. She could balance a little better like this, but she still had to keep the muscles in her core and thighs engaged to keep from falling.

"Good girl. I love you, Rebecca."

She sighed, her insides going all gooey at the words. Two months, and she still wasn't used to hearing them. "I love you, too, Nick."

"Who?"

She bit her lips to stifle the grin. He was frowning again, his brow furrowed so he looked stern and grumpy at her breach in protocol. But his eyes were laughing, and the approval there sparkled brighter than the fireworks on the fourth of July. "I love you, too, Daddy."

"Bad girl," he chided, still stern, and slipped his hand between her legs.

She stiffened when he stroked her pussy, his fingers slipping over her labia and around her clit before settling once again at the tender entrance. "Daddy, please."

"Such pretty begging," he drawled, and his finger dipped inside her, a little farther than before. But it still wasn't enough. "Again."

"Please, Daddy." She fought not to squirm on his lap, knowing how precarious her perch was. "Please can I come?"

"No," he said mildly, and pushed deep.

"Oh, fuck." Her pussy spasmed and her clit pulsed with need. She was tight and engorged and his finger was big and rough, and even though she was so wet she was practically dripping on the floor, he had to work to get inside her.

"Stay still," he warned as her hips jerked, and she fought to obey even though every instinct she had was screaming at her to move. He pulled out, leaving her empty and wanting and hanging on the edge.

"Please," she said again, her face hot and her heart pounding.

"Poor love," he crooned, and slid his fingers up and over her clit. He didn't touch it directly, no doubt aware that the slightest touch would push her over the edge. Instead, he circled it slowly, almost delicately. "You want some cock, baby? A nice, thick cock to fill you up?"

"Yes, please, Daddy," she panted, knowing it couldn't possibly be that easy.

"You gonna take what I give you?" he asked, still circling her clit.

"Yes, Daddy." Her hips were surging now, trying to follow his finger. "Please."

"Where do you want it?"

"What?" she gasped, not understanding.

"Do you want it here, in this needy, greedy pussy?" he asked, sliding his finger down to probe her slick opening again. He pumped into her once, twice, then pulled out. Her groan of disappointment was cut off when he moved his fingers back to nudge the plug. "Or do you want it in this needy, greedy asshole?"

She would've answered him, but he wrapped his fingers around the base of the plug and pulled, and the words died on a choked wail. Her asshole was still slick with lube, which meant he could pull the plug out of her without too much effort or pain, but he stopped before it was all the way out and held it there.

"Oh, shit." Rebecca breathed in heavy pants and tried to ride the wave of sensation. The plug was half in and half out of her ass, forcing her sphincter to stretch around the widest part of the toy. It burned, the muscle spasming around the plug as her body struggled to adjust to the new sensation, and every little twinge of pain made her pussy pulse in pleasure.

"Well?" he asked, and she struggled through the fog of lust to remember the question. "Which is it going to be?"

She shook her head, her hair falling into her face. She could barely see him through the curtain of it, but if she lifted a hand to move it out of the way she'd probably fall on her ass. "I don't know."

"Too bad you have to choose," he mused, a sort of malicious glee in the twist of his lips. "If there was another Dom here, someone who could slide his cock into that snug ass while I take this pretty cunt…"

The imagine conjured up by his words was so arousing she thought she might come on the spot, and when he shoved the plug back home and jammed his thumb into her cunt, it was almost her undoing. "Daddy!"

"Don't you come," he warned, pumping his thumb into her pussy.

Her fingers dug into his knees as she panted, trying to hold off the inevitable. If he didn't stop touching her, the orgasm was going to happen. He knew it, the bastard. He'd learned her body well over the last two months, and he could almost always tell when she was about to pass the point of no return. Most of the time he'd stop to give her a moment to regroup and collect herself, but sometimes he wouldn't. He'd keep going, even when it meant she wouldn't be able to keep from coming no matter how badly she tried to obey.

Which was the point of this little game. Nick wasn't interested in high protocol D/s, but he did like to torture her, and denying her orgasm—or punishing her for one—definitely fell into that category. The 'punishment' for coming without permission was never anything horrible, but it would definitely be something she didn't like. It had to be, or the rule would be meaningless.

There was a lot of room between too much and not enough, and her Daddy, it turned out, had a mean streak.

"Don't you fucking come," he said again, and let go of her ass to grab the chain attached to the clamps. He exerted a steady, slow pressure, pulling forward and down.

She lurched toward him, moving on instinct to mitigate the sudden, sharp pain in her nipples. The action drove his thumb hard into her pussy, her clit connected with the base of his hand, and that was all it took.

"Oh, no," she moaned, looking up into his face just in time to see the blaze of triumph in his eyes. Then the spasms hit, her ass clamping down on the pug and her pussy on his thumb, pleasure rolling through her in waves, drowning her in an ocean of sensation. He let go of the chain to grab her hip, keeping her steady as she jerked and trembled in his lap, but then he ducked his head, picked up the chain in his teeth and leaned back. It hurt like fire, like electrified needles under her skin, but the pain mingled so completely with the pleasure coursing through her body that it seemed she couldn't have one without the other.

And when the pleasure finally faded and she slumped against him, sweaty and spent, the pain was still there to remind her that it wasn't over.

Chapter Four

Nick gave the chain a final tug then spat it out, dropping it so it hung wetly against her abdomen. Her breasts were heaving, her nipples dark red inside the clamps.

"Bad girl," he growled. "Bad, slutty girl. You know better than to come without Daddy's permission, don't you?"

She nodded, her hair hanging forward to curtain her face. "Yes, Daddy."

"I can't hear you," he said, and lifted his hand from her hip to slap her breast. "What was that?"

"Yes, Daddy," she cried out, tears springing to her eyes. He knew all the feel-good chemicals that only moments ago were flooding her body to turn pain into pleasure had begun to fade, and from the way she flinched that smack had hurt.

"What are you?" he asked, and pulled his hand from between her thighs to slap the other breast.

She licked her lips. "A bad girl."

"That's right," he agreed. He lifted his damp hand to her face, and though his fingers were gentle, she stiffened, making him hesitate. Face slapping wasn't a hard no for her, but it would take the scene from low stakes and playful to something much more serious, and after a physically exhausting day, he wasn't sure she was in the head space to handle it.

"Yellow," she said before he could move.

His fingers stilled on her cheek, his eyes narrowing. "Tell me."

"Don't slap my face," she said, her voice ragged. "Too much."

He smiled softly and cupped her jaw, swiping at her tears with his fingertips. His thumb skimmed her mouth, smearing it with the slick juices from her cunt. "I wasn't going to, love, but thank you for telling me."

She sighed, relief lighting her eyes. "Thank you, Daddy."

"You're welcome," he murmured, still petting her face. Then he tightened his fingers on her jaw. "Now take my cock out."

Her eyes dipped down between them to the bulge in his jeans. She lifted her hands from his knees, wincing as she flexed her fingers. She'd been holding on to him so tightly that he wondered if she might have left bruises on him for once.

The thought made him smile as she reached for his waistband, then he grabbed her waist with both hands to steady her as the shifting of her weight almost sent her tumbling off his lap.

He lifted her up and put his legs closer together before setting her down again. "Better?"

She nodded. "Better."

"Good. Continue, please," he instructed, and she reached for his waistband again.

The jeans he wore were his favorites, soft from hundreds of washings, the buttonhole on the top fastening loose enough that even in a seated position, she didn't have to fight to get it undone. Three seconds later, she had his cock out, hot and thick in her hand.

"No underwear?" she asked, curling her fingers around him and stroking him hard, the way he liked it. "Slutty Daddy."

His answering grin was wolfish. "There's a condom in my pocket. Get it out."

She blinked at him, her soft gray eyes clouding in confusion. "Why?"

She was on birth control, and they'd both been tested recently so they could stop using condoms. They'd been going without for almost a month, and he waited for her to realize that he would only be planning to use a condom for one reason.

Her eyes widened as the light dawned. "Oh."

"I gave you a chance to decide," he reminded her, his eyes narrowing when she didn't move. "Condom, baby girl. Now."

She fumbled in his pocket for the little packet, letting go of his shaft to open it and roll the condom on, her fingers shaking. He let her fumble through it, watching her with a smirk his lips, his hands on her waist to keep her steady. When the condom was in place, he lifted a single, imperious eyebrow. "Lube."

She looked around for the small bottle, finally locating it on the coffee table behind her. She had to twist and stretch to reach it, her breasts swaying enticingly. He'd have loved to reach up and play with them, to see how well she performed her task with the distraction. But his grip on her waist was keeping her from falling, so he shelved that idea for another time.

She used a generous hand, coating his latex-covered cock so it gleamed. Task accomplished, she capped the bottle and dropped it to the floor.

"Take the plug out."

She shook her head. "You do it."

"Excuse me?"

She chewed her lip. "Please, Daddy?"

"Better," he allowed, fighting to keep the smile off his face. She was so damn cute. "But no. Kneel up, reach back, and pull it out. Now."

She hesitated a moment, and he waited to see what she would do. In the last two months she'd gotten to know his style of play well, and while he tended toward playful, one thing he wouldn't tolerate was topping from the bottom. He rarely rescinded an order, only doing so if safety was a factor, or if he thought of a better way to accomplish the goal at hand. If she stalled, he'd simply punish her for the disobedience, and when he was done, she'd still have to pull the plug out herself.

He waited patiently for her to make her decision, wondering which way she would go, and was pleased when she shifted in his lap, planting her knees on the cushion on either side of his legs, and knelt up.

He moved his hands, sliding them from her waist to her ass, and dug his fingers in to pull her cheeks apart. She shivered, her eyelashes fluttering as a look of intense pleasure crossed her face, and he had to bite back a laugh.

"Now, baby girl," he said, a warning edge in his voice, and she jolted back to reality.

She reached back, biting her lower lip as she stared into his eyes. She fumbled for a minute, then gritted her teeth and pulled.

"Breathe," Nick reminded her when she stiffened, waiting patiently while she battled both the lube-slick plug and her own body. She paused, panting, her eyes locked on his.

"Daddy," she whined, shaking in his arms, a plea for mercy in her wide gray eyes.

"If I have to yank that plug out, you won't sit or come for a week," he warned.

That got her moving. She let out a careful breath and pulled, a groan tumbling from her lips as the plug came free.

"Good girl," he praised with a satisfied smirk, and shifted his hands to her waist again. "Put it on the coffee table."

He held her steady while she leaned back to obey, then lifted her up. "Put your feet on the chair and squat."

He was unsurprised when she froze, discomfort twisting her face. She hated this position. She thought it was inelegant, but she couldn't take him anally any other way when she was on top. When he was in her cunt, she could ride him using her knees for balance and leverage all day long, but the way she had to tilt her pelvis forward to get the angle right for anal also made it too awkward and uncomfortable to stay on her knees.

He could've turned her around—the angle with reverse cowgirl worked better—but he wanted to see her face.

When she continued to hesitate, he narrowed his eyes. "Who am I, Rebecca?"

She swallowed, her eyes locked on his. "Daddy. My Daddy."

"And who are you?"

"Daddy's girl. Daddy's slut."

"Then get my dick in your ass. Now."

Her face flamed, but she moved, grabbing his shoulders for leverage. She got her feet under her and scooted forward, inching her feet along the cushion on either side of his legs until they were near his hips. He slid forward so his butt was at the very edge of the seat, and dropped one hand to his erection. Holding it straight up in the air, he used the other to guide her down.

"There we go," he told her, tracking her progress as she descended. The wet tip of his cock brushed her left butt cheek, and he guided her over until it settled against her asshole. "Straight down, now."

She drew in a breath and let it out slowly as she obeyed. Her asshole gave way with a gentle push, the plug having stretched her out. But he was bigger than the plug, and she tensed when he popped through the tight ring of muscle. He waited while she panted through the discomfort, enjoying the flutters and spasms on the head of his cock. Then she took a deep breath and lowered herself another inch.

"Daddy," she whined, her fingers digging into his shoulders. "It hurts."

"I know, baby," he told her, his voice soothing and unyielding. He gripped her waist with one hand and held his shaft steady with the other. "You're being such a good slut for Daddy."

Her cheeks flushed, her lips curving into a smile.

"Keep going," he urged, and dragged her down another inch.

Slowly, carefully, she lowered herself down, gratitude and resentment mingling with the pain in her eyes. He knew she found it easier to submit when he held her down or tied her down or put her in the positions he wanted, because then all the control was his, and she didn't have to do anything but take it. He loved those moments, because there was beauty in her complete surrender. But there was also beauty in the times, like now, when he directed her to do as he wished, forcing her to inflict the pain she both craved and feared, with nothing more than the desire to please him urging her forward.

Well. That, and an orgasm.

When her cheeks finally made contact with his thighs and his cock was fully embedded in her ass, she was shaking so hard that he was surprised her teeth weren't rattling. Her hands dug into his shoulders, and she was panting, every breath stirring the hair that fell across his forehead. She was gripping his cock tightly, a slick, hot fist, the smooth muscles rippling along his length.

He looked away from her face, down to her pussy, which, thanks to the tilt of her hips and the spread of her thighs, was clearly visible. She was soaking wet and bright pink, her inner labia flowered open so he could see the darker red of her open hole. Her ass rippled around his cock again, and her cunt visibly flexed in response.

"Greedy fucking cunt," he ground out, and lifted his gaze to her face in time to see her cheeks flush even darker. Her eyes were glassy, her lips parted and wet. Despite coming once, she was already close to another orgasm.

"Look at you," he said, making sure to inject a thin note of disappointment into his voice. He wasn't really angry – on the contrary, his goal in any given scene was to give her as many orgasms as possible. He'd only instituted the *no coming without permission* rule after she'd made it clear that she enjoyed being a 'bad girl' every now and then. It was part of the game, and treated as such.

But that didn't mean he could half-ass it, so he hardened his tone. "You already came once, and here you are begging to come again. Aren't you?"

She shook her head, her midnight hair slithering over her shoulders and across her breasts. "No, Daddy. I promise."

"Don't lie to me," he said sharply, and slapped her open cunt.

She jerked in his lap, letting out a scream that made him grateful he'd had the loft soundproofed when he'd moved in. Her ass tightened on his dick, making him grind his teeth to hold back his own orgasm.

When he was sure he could speak again without croaking, he lifted his hand, making sure she could see it, and said, "Try again, baby girl. Do you want to come again?"

Fear shimmered in her eyes as she stared first at his hand, poised to strike, then back at his face. "Please."

He shook his head. "Not the question I asked. One more chance."

Her breath came out in a sob and she nodded. "Yes."

"Yes, what?"

"Yes, I want to come again." Her hips rolled, as though by saying the words she could make it so. "Please, Daddy. Please can I come again?"

"No," he said cruelly, and slapped her pussy again.

She was still screaming when he grabbed her hips and dragged her up his cock, then dropped her back down again. Her eyes popped wide, shock and pain in their shining depths, and he did it again.

On the third drag and drop she picked up the beat, using her leg muscles and her grip on his shoulders to pull herself up and drop herself back down, fucking herself on his invading length. She was so slick, so hot and tight, that he knew he wouldn't last long. Which was good, because neither would she—her ass was rippling on his cock, her eyes unfocused and heavy. If he didn't hurry up, she was going to beat him there again.

"Don't you fucking come," he said, and in a desperate move, grabbed her hips and jerked her down. "This isn't for you—do you understand me? If you come again before I tell you, I'll beat your ass blue."

Her eyes were glazed and unfocused as she bounced up and down on his cock like a rag doll, breasts swaying heavily against her chest. "I can't," she managed, and the words sounded like they were being shaken out of her. "Please. Please."

"Wait," he demanded, his hips lurching upward, chasing his orgasm. "Wait."

He hammered into her from below, his grunts mingling with her whimpers. His balls were drawn tight, his cock hard and throbbing in the velvet sheath of her ass. He was so close…

She lifted her head to look him in the eye, tears shimmering. "Please come in my ass, Daddy," she begged, and that pushed him over the edge.

He arched hard, pushing himself into her as deep as he could go, resenting the barrier of the latex. He wanted to flood her ass with his come, make her bend over just so he could watch it drip out of her. The image was so clear in his head as he came, spilling himself into the condom, that he could all but feel it.

He fucked her through his orgasm, watching her through blurry eyes. She was biting her lip so hard she'd drawn blood, and tears were sliding down her cheeks in silvery streams. He had a speech planned—how good slutty girls got what they wanted, and how proud he was of her for holding off—but the orgasm sucked the words right out of his head, so all that came out of his mouth was a guttural, "Good girl. Your turn."

She peeled a hand off his shoulder to reach for her clit, fingers shaking with need. She jerked at the first touch, the high-pitched whine he loved slipping out as her ass tightened on his still-hard cock. She began to convulse, her hips jerking on him as the pleasure hit, and he had just enough wit left to reach for the clamps still holding her nipples prisoner.

She was too caught up in her orgasm to notice when he took them off, but a moment later, when the blood rushed back into the abused nubs, she noticed with a howl. She shook and screamed and moaned and cried, caught in a maelstrom of sensation, and when it was over, she fell against his chest like all her bones had turned to mush.

He wrapped his arms around her, cuddling her close. He knew he needed to get up, to deal with the condom and get both of them cleaned up. She needed some water, and a soak in the tub would help ease any soreness she'd be dealing with tomorrow, but she felt so good in his arms, warm and solid and *right,* that for the moment he was content to stay there in the fading evening light and hold her.

After a moment her breathing began to even out, and she stirred. He loosened his hold, shifting so she could move easier, and pressed his lips to her damp brow. "All right?"

She sighed, her breath gusting over his throat. "Mmm."

He smiled into her hair. Rebecca had a tendency to fade out after a scene, something he'd had to get used to over the last few months. It wasn't unusual for a submissive to need to regroup after an intense physical experience, but Rebecca was the only one he'd known who did it almost every time. He'd stopped being alarmed by it, but it always made him feel protective.

Since she was responsive—even if that response didn't consist of actual words—she probably wasn't going to go to sleep on him. He tightened his arms around her and started to sit up, intending to carry her to the bedroom, but her fingers dug into his shirt and she burrowed into his neck. "Can we just stay here for a minute?"

"Sure," he murmured, and eased back into the chair, wincing a little as his back muscles twinged in protest. He hadn't notice before, but now that his blood had cooled, he was realizing just how uncomfortable this position was.

He scooted backward, sighing with relief when he was able to relax against the chair. He tried to be careful, but she got bounced around in the scooting, and after a moment she tilted her head back to look at him.

He looked down at her, smiling as tenderness welled up inside him. She hadn't bothered with makeup for moving day, so there were no streaks of mascara or smeared lipstick on her face. But tears had left silvery tracks on her skin, and her eyes were heavy-lidded and swollen. Her lips were puffy and red from being caught in her teeth, and her hair had gotten tangled.

It was a far cry from the polished, put-together image she normally presented, and he'd never found her more beautiful.

Some of what he was thinking must have shown on his face, because her eyes softened and her lips curved. "So, that's this room christened."

That startled a laugh out of him. "We've fucked in this room before."

"Yeah, but not while I was living here."

"Oh, is that the criterion?"

"Mmm." She rubbed her cheek on his shoulder. "I don't want to move, but this is starting to get uncomfortable."

She still had her feet planted on the chair seat on either side of his hips, her knees nearly level with his armpits. "Okay, hang on to me."

She wrapped her arms around his neck. "Ready."

"Up we go," he said and stood, his hands under her butt to support her. He began walking toward the bedroom, trying to jostle her as little as possible. He was still buried in her ass, though between his dick softening and the walking he wasn't going to stay there long, and he wondered vaguely if he'd be able to make it to the bathroom before the condom fell off. He hoped so—he wasn't a fan of scrubbing come stains out of the rug.

He made it to the bathroom and eased her down to sit on the rim of the tub, making sure she was steady before he stepped away to deal with the condom. Behind him, the squeak of the taps was followed by the rush of water, and when he turned back, she was leaning forward, holding her hand under the faucet.

She was here, and not just for the night. Knowing he'd be waking up next to her every morning filled him with a deep sense of satisfaction, and suddenly he felt giddy as a child on Christmas morning.

"Hey."

She turned to him with sleepy eyes. "What are you smiling at?"

"You," he said simply, and crossed the room to draw her to her feet. He brushed her hair away from her eyes before cradling her face in his hands. "Here, in my house."

"Our house," she corrected with a smile, and wound her arms around his waist.

"Our house," he agreed, and bent his head to lay his lips on hers. "Welcome home."

Chapter Five

Rebecca woke the next morning when Nick slid out of bed, so early it was still dark outside. "You okay?" she mumbled, still half asleep.

"I'm going to get in a workout before I head to the office," he told her, his voice barely above a whisper. He stroked a hand over her hair. "Go back to sleep."

"'Kay," she sighed, and closed her eyes on his chuckle.

When she opened them again, the room was just beginning to fill with sunlight. She stretched, reaching up to the padded, tufted headboard of Nick's king-sized bed with a groan. She'd been reluctant to relegate her queen to the guest room—the wood and metal headboard was perfect for bondage, after all—but Nick had convinced her that his headboard was more kink-friendly than it appeared at first glance. The seemingly decorative copper rings attached to the buttons were actually quite functional, a fact that Nick had demonstrated to her on several occasions.

She flicked a ring, smiling when it jangled musically, then turned at the sound of footsteps. Nick strolled in from the bathroom, shirtless with a towel slung around his shoulders, his dress slacks low on his hips. He'd shaved, his face and neck red where he'd tidied up around the beard, and his hair was still damp.

He smiled when she sat up. "Morning, sleepyhead."

"Hi." She let the blankets fall to her waist as he crossed the room, and tilted her face up for his kiss. "Mmm. Did you have a cinnamon roll for breakfast?"

"Mouthwash," he said, and kissed her one more time before straightening to cross to the closet.

"You're the only person I know who hates the taste of spearmint," she said on a yawn, and leaned back against the pillows.

"Clearly there are more of us," he called back from the depths of the closet, his voice muffled, "or there wouldn't be cinnamon mouthwash."

"Maybe there are people who just love cinnamon."

He emerged with a crisp white shirt in one hand and a suit jacket that matched his gray pants in the other. "Better than people who love spearmint."

She snuggled against the pillows to watch him dress. It was oddly hypnotic, and she found herself drifting toward sleep again.

"Are you falling back asleep?" he asked, amused, and she forced her eyes back open.

"I'm tired," she told him. "I moved this weekend."

"I know. I carried all the boxes."

"Not all the boxes," she reminded him. "James and Jack helped. And I had to unpack them all."

"Amanda and Sadie offered to help with that," he pointed out.

"I know, but I wanted to do it myself." She wrinkled her nose. "Do you think they were offended?"

He shifted so his eyes met hers in the mirror. "I think they understood. If Sadie was offended, she'll tell you."

"That's true," Rebecca conceded. Her friend and former neighbor was nothing if not brutally honest. "I'm having lunch with her, so I guess I'll find out."

He tucked in his shirt. "What else do you have planned for your day off?"

"Organizing, though I got most of that done. I might try to get a haircut."

He turned away from the mirror with a frown. "You want to cut your hair?"

"Just a trim," she said idly. "I'm starting to get split ends."

He grunted at that, which she took to mean he had no idea what split ends were—or didn't care.

His shirt all buttoned and tucked in, he picked up his jacket and slipped it on. "I don't have anything unusual on my schedule today, so I should be home on time."

"Okay. Are we going to the St. Patrick's Day thing at James and Amanda's?"

"I'd planned on it. Why, do you not want to?"

"It's not that," she told him as he sat on the edge of the bed to pull on his shoes. "I just don't have any green fetish wear. I might see if Sadie can go shopping with me."

"Don't let her talk you into anything with glitter. I swear I'm still finding red sparkles from your Valentine's Day outfit in my hair."

"Trust me, I am never doing glitter again." He wasn't the only one still finding it in odd places. The esthetician who'd done her bikini wax last week had been very confused.

"Good." He stood, then bent down to give her a kiss. "Enjoy your day off, love."

She reached up to toy with the open collar of his shirt. He hardly ever wore a tie unless he had outside meetings scheduled, and he'd gotten into the habit of leaving a few of them at work so he didn't have to put one on until the last minute. The skin of his throat was warm, and he smelled like the beard oil she'd gotten him for Christmas. "Are you sure you don't want to take the day off? We could christen another room."

"Don't tempt me," he growled, stealing another kiss before straightening. "Nate's crawling up my ass about finalizing this merger, and I don't want to leave Kit to deal with him alone."

Rebecca frowned. Kit was the assistant Nick had hired when she'd quit, and they'd become friends during the two weeks that Rebecca had stayed on to train her. She was friendly and personable as well as smart and efficient, and she'd quickly integrated herself into the tight-knit office. Everyone seemed to adore her, except for Nate, Nick's twin brother and business partner. For some reason nobody could fathom, he was the lone exception. "Are they still not getting along?"

He shot her a look as he picked up his wallet and keys from the dresser. "Not getting along is an understatement. He won't even come to my office at this point, and three of his team leads threatened to quit if he didn't stop being, and I quote, a 'grumpy motherfucker'."

"And to think, you used to be the grumpy one," she teased.

"That was because I was sexually frustrated," he reminded her.

"Maybe that's Nate's problem, too," she ventured, and shrugged when he stared at her. "Stranger things have happened."

"I hope to God that's not true," he said, a familiar scowl on his face as he shoved his wallet into his pocket. "I am not losing another assistant to unrequited lust."

"Excuse me," she said primly, "but your lust is fully requited now. You're welcome."

He grinned. "Speaking of which, I believe you have a punishment coming."

"I'm not sure I know what you're talking about, Sir," she replied, still prim and wincing on the inside. She should've known he wouldn't forget.

He raised an eyebrow. "Want to make it two punishments?"

"You're a mean Daddy," she decided, pouting harder when he laughed.

He crossed to the bed to kiss her goodbye, lingering over it until she was squirming. "Be good today."

"I will," she promised.

"That means no masturbating."

"What?" She pulled back to blink at him. "Why?"

"Because I said so."

"So mean." She hadn't been thinking about getting herself off until he'd forbidden it, damn him.

"Rebecca," he warned.

"Yes, Daddy," she conceded with a sigh. "No masturbating."

"That's my good girl," he said, and smiled when she shivered. "I love you."

"I love you, too."

He pressed a last kiss to her mouth, then straightened and headed for the door. "Tell Sadie I said hello."

"Will do," she called after him, sighing a little when she heard the front door close behind him.

"No masturbating," she muttered, and got out of bed. It was a good thing she'd bathed last night, because avoiding the hand-held shower wand was suddenly very necessary.

* * * *

By the time Sadie rang the bell, Rebecca had managed to cross most of the things off her to-do list. Nick had given her carte blanche to change the apartment any way she wanted, and she'd taken him at his word, rearranging the furniture to her liking and hanging her art on the walls. She'd given away her couch, agreeing with Nick that his sectional was both newer and more suited to the large open space, but she'd warmed up the slate-gray fabric with colorful cushions and her Tiffany lamps on the dark wood end tables.

The knickknacks she'd collected over the years sat on the coffee table and bookshelves, and her brightly colored dishes graced the open shelves in the kitchen. Nick had decorated mostly in shades of gray, and it was remarkable how a few splashes of color brightened up the place.

"Starting to come together," she decided, and went to answer the door.

"You brought Thai," she said, inhaling deeply as she eyed the takeout cartons in her friend's hands. "Thank God."

Sadie planted a smacking kiss on Rebecca's cheek before shoving the food at her. "Here, take it so I can get out of this ridiculous coat."

Rebecca closed the door and obliged, then stepped back as Sadie fought her way out of the enormous parka. "Is it that cold out?"

"Yes." Sadie dropped the coat on the hook by the door and turned, tugging her purple sweater back down over her hips. Her strawberry-blonde hair was down, the baby-fine strands sticking up from the static electricity produced by her struggle with the coat. "I was going to have a beer with lunch, but now I think I might need hot chocolate."

"How about boozy hot chocolate?" Rebecca suggested, leading the way into the kitchen.

"Sold."

They divvied up the food and made the drinks, then settled in at the breakfast bar to eat.

"The place looks really good," Sadie observed, swiveling on her stool to take in the changes Rebecca had made to Nick's utilitarian decorating scheme. "But you need a dining room table."

"I know. We're going shopping for one together this week."

Sadie's face twisted in a grimace. "Really?"

"And by 'shopping together', of course what I mean is 'I will find a store with several options to show Nick because if I try to get him to go to more than one place, he will start to argue we should just get a pool table, which was his plan before I moved in'."

"Of course. Other than that, things are good?"

"Things are good." Rebecca sipped her hot chocolate and promptly choked. "Jesus, how much whiskey did you put in here?"

"It's less 'hot chocolate with whiskey' and more 'whiskey with hot chocolate'," Sadie admitted.

"No shit." Rebecca took another sip. "Once you get past the shock, it's pretty awesome."

"Kind of like me," Sadie said, and Rebecca laughed.

They plowed through lunch, chatting between mouthfuls of Pad Thai about mutual friends and the upcoming St. Patrick's Day party, and when they were finished, took another round of whiskey with hot chocolate to the living room.

"So, you've been living together for twenty-four hours now," Sadie began, curling up in a corner of the sofa. "Any regrets?"

Rebecca huffed out a laugh. "Not so far. Although, apparently, I need to keep some towels in the living room."

"Jizz rags?" Sadie guessed, and waggled her brows.

"No. Well, yes. But I was thinking more about how I ended up eating dinner naked last night, sitting on a sofa pillow on the floor."

Sadie froze. "It's not the one I'm sitting on, is it?"

"No," Rebecca said with a laugh. "And even if it was, I had my robe under me."

"Good call. Why exactly did you eat dinner naked?"

"We're figuring out the parameters of our D/s, and Nick said he wanted to see how it felt."

Sadie's eyes widened. "I thought you didn't want a D/s relationship outside of sex."

"I didn't think I did," Rebecca admitted. "And neither did Nick. But I like clear boundaries, clear expectations, and Nick thought having some basic rules spelled out would help. So, we're trying it out."

"So? How did it feel to eat naked?"

Rebecca thought for a moment. "A little strange, but not bad. I was mostly worried about getting crumbs in my crotch."

"Ew."

"I know, right?"

"What other rules do you have?" Sadie prompted.

"Most of them only apply during sex, but they're pretty basic. No topping from the bottom, he's in charge, yadda yadda."

Sadie grinned. "Please tell me you actually say 'yadda yadda' to Nick."

"Sorry to disappoint you, but no. I like being able to sit down."

"Wimp."

"Hey, we can't all be brats," Rebecca pointed out.

"I *am* one of a kind," Sadie mused.

"Anyway, we're trying to see how much D/s we're comfortable with in every day. We both have full-time jobs, and neither of us wants a twenty-four-seven arrangement. I think we'll probably be trying different things for the next little while until we find the right balance."

"More naked dinners," Sadie said with a grin.

"Probably. It did make me feel more submissive, but I don't know how much of that was the nudity and how much was the rest of it."

"I wondered when we were going to get to the good stuff." Sadie wiggled in her seat, her eyes bright over her mug. "Tell me."

"I think Nick wants to have a threesome."

Sadie rolled her eyes with a smirk. "What, like a 'two submissives at his beck and call' thing? Typical."

"No, like a 'two Doms to drive me wild' thing."

Sadie choked on her hot chocolate. "Okay, less typical. For sex, or for a scene?"

"Both, I think."

"I need a minute," Sadie said, and closed her eyes for a moment. "Okay. Do you want a threesome?"

"In theory? I love the idea. The two-man tag team is actually one of my go-to fantasies."

Sadie nodded soberly. "Uh-huh, I'm with you."

"But in practice..." She chewed her lip. "I don't know, I just never thought about making it real."

"And now that you're thinking about it?"

"It seems really hot," she admitted with a laugh. "Have you ever had a threesome?"

"A couple of times."

Rebecca waited, but for once Sadie stayed silent. "And?"

"And it was hot, but also kind of awkward, to be honest." Sadie shifted in her seat, her frown contemplative. "And the sex wasn't great."

"Really?"

"I have a hard time coming under the best of circumstances, and splitting my focus really didn't help."

Rebecca winced. "I'm sorry."

She shrugged. "It was when I was in college, and nobody knows how to fuck in college. Also, I hadn't figured out I was kinky yet, or at least not all the way, and I was struggling with a lot of shame about my sexuality in general. Hard to come with all that in my head.

"But that's me," she went on, the familiar smirk back on her face as she looked at Rebecca. "We're talking about you. Are you going to do it?"

"I don't know. Honestly, I don't even know if Nick was just bringing it up to mess with me, because that's what Doms do—"

Her friend nodded sagely. "That is what they do."

"—or if he's serious about it."

"You didn't ask him?"

"I've learned that it's best if we have those conversations while we're *not* naked," Rebecca said drily. "Less chance of it devolving into foreplay. That man can turn anything into a segue to sex."

"Lucky you," Sadie said with a laugh.

"I'll talk to him about it when we're both fully dressed, and we'll see where it goes. In the meantime, I have other things to worry about."

"Like?"

"I came without permission last night," Rebecca sighed. "Which means I have a punishment coming."

"Ouch." Sadie's expression was sympathetic. "Did he tell you how?"

Rebecca shook her head. "He likes to mess with me."

"It's what they do," Sadie said with such sorrowful sympathy that Rebecca snorted.

"It won't be *too* bad, though, right?" Sadie asked.

"No. He mostly made it a rule just to torture me, so the punishment is usually more of the same. But it'll be awful enough to make me not want to break the rule. And I bet he'll make it public."

Sadie's eyes went round. "Like at the supermarket?"

Rebecca laughed until she thought her ribs would break. "I meant like at a public party."

"Oh." Sadie frowned slightly. "Do you not like public play?"

"I'm fine with public play," Rebecca explained, her cheeks going warm. "Public punishment is a whole other ball of wax."

"Would he do that to you?"

"In a heartbeat," Rebecca said with a sigh. "He's diabolical."

"And you love it."

"I really do," Rebecca said with a laugh. "My brain is a weird place sometimes."

"Girl, same."

Rebecca grinned. "What are you doing the rest of today?"

"Nothing, actually. I had three clients this morning, and my afternoon is clear."

"Want to go shopping for a St. Paddy's Day outfit with me? I have to get something green, or I'm going to get pinched black and blue at the party before Nick even gets a chance to punish me."

"Oh, yeah." Sadie grimaced. "I hate that pinching thing. It's so fucking junior high."

"Right? Like, we're grown-ups at a play party, so just spank me already."

Sadie snickered. "I'm going to borrow that line."

Rebecca shook her head. "I don't know how you don't get hung from the ceiling and beaten like a pinata."

"Don't give anyone any ideas." Sadie stood, plucked Rebecca's empty mug out of her hand, and headed for the kitchen. "Come on, let's go shopping. I'm thinking slutty leprechaun for me, and a green G-string and shamrock pasties for you."

"Keep thinking," Rebecca advised, and went to get her coat.

* * * *

A week later, Rebecca was in the dining room, naked and sweaty and still a little breathless, frowning at their new table. "I don't know if I love it."

"You weren't complaining a minute ago," Nick reminded her from the depths of the refrigerator. "Want a beer?"

She resisted the urge to roll her eyes. While not expressly against the rules—which they were still working out—she and her backside had discovered that Nick found eyerolling to be particularly disrespectful. "A minute ago, I was facedown over it, coming my brains out. And no, thank you."

Nick shut the fridge and came around the island, popping the cap off his beer bottle. His pants hung loosely on his hips, zipped but not buttoned, and he hadn't bothered to put his shirt back on. He touched the cold bottle to her nipple and grinned when she squeaked. "You're welcome."

"I'm serious," she said even as she laughed, edging away from the beer bottle. "Doesn't it look off to you?"

"It looks like a table." He lifted the bottle for a long drink. "You loved it in the store."

"I know, but..." She tapped her lip. It was a beautiful piece, and just what she'd been looking for, but something wasn't right. She looked up at the industrial metal light fixture that hung from the tall ceiling, the only thing besides the table that defined the space as a dining area. "Maybe it's the lighting."

Nick looked up. "You want to change the light?"

"I think so." She tilted her head to study it. "Maybe something warmer. Still modern, but less industrial looking."

"Okay," Nick said agreeably, and tipped back his beer.

She glanced at him in exasperated amusement. "Do you have an opinion about this at all?"

"Not even a little bit," he said promptly, and grinned when she huffed out a breath. "I literally don't care."

"I just want it to be right."

He shifted his beer to his other hand and slid his arm around her waist. "I know you do. And I love that you do. But I don't think my input is going to help."

She laid her head on his chest. "Probably not. You're kind of awful at this."

"Very awful," he agreed. "But I love that you're so invested in making our house a home."

She tipped her head back to smile at him. "Thanks."

"You're welcome." He lowered his head to kiss her, his hand rubbing her back as she shivered. "Cold?"

"A little." She snuggled closer, grimacing as a bit of come, cold and clammy now, slid down her leg. "And I need to clean up."

He gave her butt a firm pat. "Go do that, and get dressed."

"I don't have to stay naked?"

"No, you don't have to stay naked. But make it something I can get under easily."

"Okay." She rose on her toes for one last kiss, then hurried to the bathroom.

Five minutes later, washed and bundled up in the red cashmere robe, she came back out to find him sitting on the couch, still shirtless, remote in hand. "Aren't you cold?"

He smiled and lifted his arm so she could snuggle against him. "Nah. You want to watch a movie?"

"Sure." His bare skin was warm under her cheek, and she was relaxed and sleepy from christening the new table. "Something funny, please."

"You got it."

She let her mind wander as he searched through the options, idly combing her fingers through his chest hair. "Hey, can I ask you a question?"

"Sure." He was frowning at the screen, squinting a little at the titles. "They need to make this print bigger."

"Or you might need glasses," she pointed out, and kept her face tucked against his side so he wouldn't see her smirk.

"Smart ass," he muttered, and smacked her hip.

"Ow," she complained, rubbing at the sting. "What was that for?"

"Cheekiness," he decided, and handed her the remote. "Here, you find something."

She took it and went to the comedy heading. "Oooh, *Young Frankenstein*."

"That'll do," he decided, and took the remote to set it on the end table as the opening credits began to roll. "So?"

"So, what?"

"You said you had a question."

"Right." She hesitated a moment. Bringing it up had seemed like a good idea only moments before, but forcing the words out of her mouth was proving harder than she'd thought. "It's about the other day."

"What other day?"

"Moving day."

His attention was on the screen. "What about it?"

"Were you serious, or was it just part of the game?"

That got his attention. "Was what part of the game?"

"The idea of us having a threesome."

He picked up the remote and hit pause, then shifted on the couch so they were face to face. "What do you think?"

"I don't know. That's why I'm asking."

"You know I've done threesomes before."

She nodded. "With Cade, right?"

"Him, and a few others."

"Was it just sex, or sex and play?"

His eyes were steady and watchful. "Both. The sex ones were fun, but I like the sex and play combination more."

"Doesn't it get confusing with two Doms?"

"Not really. It takes a little planning, and a willingness to be flexible, but it can be a very fulfilling experience."

"I would think it would get, I don't know, competitive."

"Like 'who's the best Dom'?" he asked, and shook his head. "You can't think like that, or it won't work. It's not about who's better at bondage, or flogging, or whatever. It's about working together to meet the submissive's needs and deliver the best scene possible."

"Oh."

"Have you been thinking about this a lot?"

"Off and on since that night," she admitted, her cheeks warming as she looked into his eyes.

"Is it something you want to do?"

He was watching her so closely, so carefully. "I don't know. It's a fantasy of mine—you know that—but I don't know if I want to make it a reality."

"Fair enough." He reached for her hand, twining their fingers together. "Do you want me to help you figure it out?"

She blinked. "How would you do that?"

"Baby steps," he said cryptically.

"That doesn't tell me anything," she told him.

"I know," he said, and laughed softly when she scowled. "I'm not going to give you Chapter and verse, Rebecca."

"Dammit," she muttered.

"It's up to you, though," he continued, smiling. "You can keep thinking about it on your own, if you want."

She chewed on her lip, indecision gnawing at her. She'd been going in circles in her own head for a while with no clear answers, and it might be nice to get a different perspective. But she didn't fully trust the gleam in his eye.

"I have a few questions," she hedged.

"Go ahead."

"If we did something like this—and I'm not saying yes—would it change our relationship? I mean, would we be opening it up?"

"No," he said firmly. "This would be a single, one-time scene—with the option to do it again, if both of us were comfortable with it—not a change to our relationship structure. I have no interest in that."

"Me neither," she said, relieved.

"Good. What else?"

"Would it be with someone we know?"

"Yes."

"Cade?"

"He'd be my first choice. I trust him, and we work well together." He narrowed his eyes slightly. "Does that idea bother you?"

"I might feel more comfortable with a stranger," she admitted. "Someone I didn't have to see on a regular basis. We could hire a sex worker."

"If we were just talking about sex, I'd consider it. But to let another Dom top you, I need a level of trust that I'm just not going to get from a stranger."

"Oh."

He angled his head. "Do you not like Cade?"

"Oh, no! I like Cade just fine. It just might be awkward. You know, after."

"Very possible." He squeezed her hand. "But we're getting ahead of ourselves. First order of business is to find out if this is something you want to even do, yes?"

"Yes."

"Do you want my help?"

"Yes?" she said, much more cautiously.

Amusement sparkled in his clear blue eyes. "Is that a question, or an answer?"

"Well, you're sneaky," she told him. "And you like to mess with me."

"This is true," he said, smiling now.

Then she sighed. "But I trust you, and I know you wouldn't do anything to harm me, so…yes. I would like your help figuring out if this is something I truly want to do."

He leaned forward to capture her lips in a deep kiss. "Thank you for your trust."

"Baby steps, though, right?"

"Baby steps," he agreed. He tugged on the lapel of her robe. "Take this off."

"I'll be cold," she complained, even as she moved to comply.

"I'll keep you warm," he promised, and pulled her into his side again. He draped the robe over her like a blanket, his hand warm on her waist under it, then picked up the remote again. "Hey."

She lifted her head. "What?"

"I love you."

"I love you, too." She smiled at him, then pressed a kiss to his chest and snuggled back in to watch the movie.

Chapter Six

Nick stood in the small bathroom under the stairs, arms crossed over his chest, and regarded his submissive with amusement. "If you don't take it off in the next thirty seconds, baby girl, I'm going to have to rethink your punishment for tonight."

The look she shot him from under her lashes was both fuming and cajoling. "Can't you just spank me until I can't sit down for a week?"

"I could, if you'd like that on top of what I already have planned," he said agreeably, and had to stifle a laugh when her shoulders slumped. "Down to fifteen seconds."

That got her moving. She reached for the hem of her sweater dress—green, as the holiday demanded—and in a swift, ripping-off-the-bandage move, whipped it over her head. She balled it up, apparently unconcerned about wrinkles, and stuffed it into one corner of the toy bag he held. "There. Happy?"

He reached out and snagged her chin, jerking her head around so she had no choice but to meet his eyes. "Careful, there. I don't mind a bit of brat now and then, but watch yourself."

She swallowed hard, the gulp audible in the small room. "Sorry, Daddy," she whispered, her eyes wide. "I'm anxious."

"I know." He kept his fingers firm on her face. "But that attitude will not be tolerated. Am I clear?"

"Yes, Daddy."

"Good girl." He gentled his touch, skimming his fingers over her mouth before standing back to look at her. "You look beautiful."

She squirmed, delighting him. "Thank you."

Her St. Patrick's Day outfit consisted of a pair of high heels that fastened with a satin ribbon in emerald green, a matching bow in her ink black hair, and nothing in between. He'd considered letting her wear the pasties and G-string she'd bought, but as the party was being held in James and Amanda's basement, there was no need to cover up. Rebecca didn't normally mind being naked at a play party—she almost always ended up that way, no matter what she started out wearing—but having her start the party without a stitch on, while most other people would be dressed, had her off balance.

Which, of course, was the point.

"Turn for me," he instructed, pleased when she did so immediately. There were goosebumps on her skin, but despite her nudity, he didn't think she was cold. The basement was kept warm, since most if not all the attendees would end up in some state of undress before the night was out. Still, he'd keep an eye on her.

Then his gaze dropped to the new addition at the small of her back. The temporary tattoo was bright green, the lettering a flowing script that required the reader to look hard to make out the words. It had taken him a while to apply it, since he'd had to put the letters on individually and she'd kept wiggling, but he'd managed to make it look like one large, continuous piece.

He reached out, tracing one finger over the script. "Hit me, I'm Irish," he read, chuckling when she shivered, and tapped one of the arrows that flanked the words on each side, pointing to her butt. "This should help keep you warm tonight."

"My butt, anyway," she muttered, twisting to look at him over her shoulder. "Have I mentioned lately that you're diabolical, Daddy?"

"Aw, thanks for noticing, baby girl," he drawled, and took a moment to assess the anxiety in her eyes. Maybe a five or a six out of ten, he decided—enough to make this count as punishment, not enough to push her into truly scary territory. "Remember the rules?"

"Any Dom or Top can spank me, but they have to tell me first, and I have to answer 'yes, Sir,' or 'Ma'am,' or whatever honorific they go by. I have to bend over and put my hands on the floor while they do, and I have to thank them afterwards." She paused to draw in a shaky breath, then continued. "I can refuse someone, but I have to be polite, and I have to immediately come and find you to tell you why."

"Good girl. I debated not letting you refuse anyone, you know," he said, and she jerked her head around, eyes flared with alarm. "I decided against that, partly because I won't be with you every moment, and because your right to decide who touches you didn't disappear when you became my submissive."

She sagged slightly, relief and gratitude easing her expression.

"However," he said, his hand on her hip hardening, "if I find you're arbitrarily refusing people in an attempt to get out of the punishment, I will be very unhappy with you. Clear?"

She nodded. "Clear."

"Good girl." He eased his grip to a soothing caress. "Later, we'll handle the rest of your punishment.

"How much later?" she asked, completely missing the significance of the word 'we'.

"When I'm ready," he said, and watched the anxiety in her gaze kick up a notch. Some submissives enjoyed surprises, but Rebecca wasn't one of them. She did much better, especially with punishments, if she knew what to expect and when, so keeping her guessing was a very effective way to torment her.

"I want you to mingle for a while," he said. "Keep to the main room. If you need to go anywhere else—even the bathroom—come find me first. Understood?"

She rolled her shoulders like a prize fighter about to step into the ring, her mouth a tight line. Her eyes were locked on his hand, resting on the doorknob. "I understand."

"Rebecca." He waited until her wary gaze met his, then smiled. "I'm proud of you."

The fear in her eyes abated, pleasure lighting them from within as her cheeks went pink. Her shoulders relaxed, and her mouth softened. "I'm being silly, aren't I?"

"You're being you," he corrected, holding her gaze with his. "And I love you."

She smiled at him. "I love you, too."

"I know," he said with a cocky grin, just so he could watch her fight not to roll her eyes. He opened the door and gave her a solid smack on her pert ass. "Now get out there."

She sent him a cheeky pout over her shoulder as she passed, though he could see the anxiety dancing in her eyes. He waited for a moment, then followed her out.

The basement was bright and warm, the open space filled with laughter and music. About thirty people milled about, dressed in everything from fancy evening wear to leathers to nothing. There was a trio gathered at the pool table for a game, and several people perched on the sofas near the cheerfully crackling fireplace. Rebecca was about ten feet in front of him, head turning slowly as she glanced around the room. Her stiff shoulders relaxed a bit when she saw two of her friends, Sadie and Amanda, arranging snacks on a table set up across the room.

She took a step in their direction, but before she could go further, James stepped into her path.

He laid a hand on her arm, drawing her to a halt, then lifted his gaze over her head to Nick. He gave his friend a nod, which James acknowledged with a wink, then turned to face the room.

"Everyone, if I could have your attention, please."

Though he barely raised his voice, conversation immediately died down, and someone—probably Amanda, James' wife—turned down the music. Within seconds, every eye in the room was focused on James—and the naked woman next to him.

"Thank you all for coming tonight," James began, and Nick saw his fingers tighten on Rebecca's arm when she tried to subtly edge away. She halted immediately and, though her hands twitched at her sides as though she wanted to cover herself, stood still.

"As most of you likely already know, there are snacks set up at the back of the room—thank you, Amanda and Sadie—and a full bar by the pool table. You're welcome to help yourself to whatever you like, and if there's something else you need, please ask Amanda. Though as she's in puppy mode tonight, her responses are limited."

James paused as a wave of laughter went around the room, and Amanda, sitting on her haunches by the snack table, let out a happy yip, the bell on her collar jingling musically.

"As usual, the two bedrooms are available for play—we simply ask that you keep the doors open so our DMs can monitor the scenes. There are tarps and chucks in both rooms if anyone is interested in blood play, as well as sharps containers. Please be considerate of the carpets and bedding. Some of you may be happy to hear that the bathrooms are available for watersports—just please make sure your submissive is near a drain."

A cheer went up from one corner, and Nick saw a very pleased-looking Collette, her boy Sam kneeling at her feet.

"I thought you'd like that," James called out to Collette, and laughter once again flowed through the room.

"Also, as a special St. Patrick's Day treat, we have Rebecca."

Nick was watching her closely, so he saw the small jolt go through her as James called out her name. She twisted her head, no doubt looking for him. She couldn't see him without turning almost all the way around, though, and James' grip on her arm was too firm to allow it.

"Rebecca's Daddy has kindly offered her ass up for our use tonight—literally. Turn around, Rebecca."

He pulled on her arm, and she had no choice but to obey. Her eyes immediately found him, leaning against the wall ten feet behind her, and she tried to take a step forward. But James' hand and Nick's firm head shake stopped her.

"There's a message on Rebecca's back," James said, and gestured to the tattoo decorating the base of her spine while she begged Nick with her eyes to rescue her, "which entitles the reader to spank her very lovely backside. The rules are as follows—two spanks only, of whatever level you wish, with the implement of your choice. However, you may not break the skin."

Nick kept his eyes on Rebecca as James continued, forcing himself to remain impassive. Her soft gray eyes were as wide as saucers, a frantic plea in them. But her nipples were hard now, flushed with color, and the wetness on her upper thighs shone in the light.

She was scared, and she was turned on. *Perfect.*

"You must inform Rebecca of your intent to spank her," James went on, "and give her time to assume the position, which she will demonstrate now."

Rebecca blinked, darting her gaze to James. Then she was looking at Nick again, the heat in her eyes nearly as bright as the trepidation as she slowly bent forward at the waist, putting herself on display for the room. Nick knew from experience that even with her legs closed, her pussy would be visible between her thighs, and from the bright red blush riding her cheekbones, she knew it too.

James let her hang there for a moment, making sure the whole room had a clear view, then gently tugged on Rebecca's arm in a signal to stand. She popped up like a Jack-in-the-Box, hair mussed and cheeks blazing.

"She is also allowed to refuse you," James continued, and his voice hardened. "And I want to make it clear that if you fail to respect that refusal, you will be asked to leave my home, and you will not be invited back."

Nick scanned the room carefully as that announcement was made, looking for murmurs of dissatisfaction. He eased out a breath when he found nothing but agreement on the faces assembled. For the most part he trusted this community, but there were always one or two wildcards, and he'd wanted to make it clear that violating Rebecca's consent—and his—would not be tolerated. Thankfully James felt the same way, and had readily agreed to toss any violators out on their ear.

"Are there any questions?"

"Do we get more than one turn?" someone called out from the back of the room.

"Feeling greedy tonight, Joel?" James called out, raising his voice to be heard over the laughter. "If you want a second turn, see Nick. He'll decide."

Joel gave a whoop, making the room erupt into laughter again, and Nick quickly controlled his irritation. Unless he missed his guess, Joel wasn't even going to get a first turn. Rebecca didn't like the younger man much, and Nick couldn't blame her. He wasn't a bad guy, and showed potential as a Dom, but he was a bit of a showman, and arrogant with it. He'd likely grow out of it as he matured and gained more experience in the scene, but right now his play seemed to have too much braggadocio and not enough care and attention for his partner, and submissives were starting to refuse to play with him.

Nick thought the kid could do with a mentor, and James agreed. But Joel had been offended at the suggestion, and short of throwing him out, there wasn't anything they could do about it. He hadn't done anything worthy of ejection—yet—so they'd agreed the best course of action was to continue to monitor his behavior, in scene and out. If he stepped so much as a toe out of line, he'd get the boot.

"If there are no more questions," James was saying, "then I'll take my turn now. Rebecca?"

It took her a moment to pull her eyes away from Nick and look up at James. "Sir?"

"I'm going to spank you."

Rebecca nodded, her throat bobbing, and Nick could see the fine tremor in the hands she held carefully at her sides. "Yes, Sir," she said, and bent over once more.

James took his time, waiting until Rebecca's hands were on the floor in front of her. Then quickly, too quickly to give her time to prepare, delivered a stinging slap to each cheek. Her gasp of shock and pain was loud in the quiet room, and an appreciative murmur went through the crowd.

James helped her straighten, holding her steady when she wobbled slightly. "Thank you, Sir," she said dutifully, and a newbie on their first day in the dungeon would've heard the purr in her voice.

James' mouth quirked up in a smile as he skimmed a finger down her flushed cheek. "You're quite welcome, little one."

He bent to press a kiss to her disheveled hair, shooting Nick another wink, then stepped back. "Enjoy the party, everyone."

On cue the music once again filled the room, and people drifted back to their conversations. The clatter of balls sounded from the pool table as Nick approached a wide-eyed Rebecca.

As James had done, he skimmed a finger down her cheek. Her skin was warm, almost hot to the touch, and her eyes were cloudy with lust. He knew the answer, but he asked the question anyway. "What color are you, Rebecca?"

"Green," she said, the word trembling on her lips. "I'm green, Daddy."

"My beautiful girl," he murmured, and cupped her face in both hands. He kept the kiss slow, wanting to convey not just how much he desired her but how proud he was, and how much he loved her. When he lifted his head, her eyes were heavy, her pulse hammering in the hollow of her throat. "I love you."

"I love you, too," she sighed, swaying toward him.

"Careful," he cautioned, and dropped his hands to her shoulders to steady her. He held her there a moment, until some of the fog cleared from her eyes. "All right?"

She drew a deep breath and blew it out, then smiled. It was a little dreamy, and need still shone in her eyes, but she seemed to be firing on all cylinders again. "I'm good."

"That's my girl," he said approvingly, and slapped a hand on her ass. Her squeak made him grin. "Now, go do what you were told."

"Yes, Daddy," she said, a sulky pout on her mouth as she rubbed her butt.

He raised an eyebrow and tapped one finger her plump lower lip. "Keep sticking that lip out, and something might get attached to it. Like a clover clamp," he suggested, then roared with laughter when she immediately folded her lips in a tight line. He yanked her close for one more kiss, then sent her on her way with another pat on her ass.

"Go. Find me if you need me," he said, and strolled away with a grin on his face.

* * * *

An hour and a half later, Rebecca was standing in front of the fireplace. She wasn't cold, but pretending she was gave her the perfect excuse to keep her ass out of view. She'd been spanked by almost every Top in the room at this point, some of them twice, and while none of them had been too cruel, she was ready for a break.

"How's your butt feel?" Sadie asked from her perch on the hearth next to her.

"Hurts, but not too bad," she confessed, lowering her voice to minimize the chances of inadvertently challenging any nearby tops. "On a scale of one to ten, maybe a six?"

Sadie frowned in confusion, the sparkly shamrock sticker on her cheek glowing as she cocked her head. "Then why aren't you sitting?"

"Because if these Tops see me on my butt, they'll take it as a personal challenge," Rebecca replied in a near whisper. "And because I'm so wet I'll probably leave a puddle behind."

Sadie giggled, her pigtails bouncing lightly. She'd dressed for the holiday in a short green skirt that barely covered her ass, held up by rainbow suspenders. She'd gone shirtless, covering her nipples with the shamrock pasties Nick hadn't let Rebecca wear, and her usual white ankle socks and black Mary Janes had been replaced by a pair of Pleasers with sparkly gold soles and clear plastic uppers that snowed off her emerald-green toenails.

"How do you walk in those things?" Rebecca wanted to know.

"Not well," Sadie admitted, angling her foot to admire the shoes. The platform was at least three inches, the heel at least seven. "If it weren't for the ankle strap, I'd probably break my neck. I had to wear sneakers on the drive over and change when I got here."

She shook her head, making her pigtails bounce and sway. "I have such a new respect for strippers. They can actually *dance* in these things."

"I took pole dancing lessons when I lived in Texas," Rebecca said. "I thought I had decent core strength until the first class."

"Right?" Sadie laughed. "Mad respect."

"Excuse me, ladies."

Rebecca turned to smile at Kody, automatically dipping her knees in the abbreviated curtsey she'd been using all night. The older Top was shorter than Rebecca, their iron-gray hair scooped up in a short mohawk, and though their smile was kind, a hint of sadism lurked in the depths of their faded blue eyes.

"Your Grace," Rebecca murmured, remembering the honorific they had chosen. After coming out as nonbinary, Kody had tried out half a dozen titles before settling on that one, and Rebecca was pleased she'd remembered it. In her opinion, it suited them much better than the military style ones they'd started out with. Although they'd looked pretty awesome in the fatigues.

"Here to claim a spanking, little one," Kody announced, and Rebecca's gaze dropped to the leather paddle in their hand.

She had to wince. Nick had a similar paddle, the leather strap narrow and flexible, and she knew it would add an additional layer of discomfort to her already throbbing ass.

"Of course, Your Grace." She turned and bent at the waist, placing her hands on the floor by Sadie's feet.

The space around the fireplace was popular, and there were a few too many people milling around to get a decent wind-up. Still, there was a considerable amount of power behind the blows, and Kody managed to land them both in the same spot, right where her butt met her thighs, dead in the middle. And since she'd forgotten to clamp her thighs tightly together, her swollen labia took part of the impact.

Rebecca stayed bent over for a moment, her breath coming in pants, until the stars faded from her eyes. Slowly, one hand planted on Sadie's knee for balance, she straightened and turned to face Kody once again.

"Thank you, Your Grace," she managed, her butt throbbing and her pussy tingling.

"You're welcome," Kody replied, amusement and a hint of concern in their voice as they watched Rebecca try to regain her composure. "Do you want me to help you sit?"

"No!" Rebecca burst out in panic, the mere thought of sitting sending a shiver of pain through her system. Then she took a careful breath and spoke more calmly. "I mean, no, thank you. I'll be fine."

Kody's eyes were coolly assessing, though a hint of the humor that had leapt in them at Rebecca's outburst still lingered. "I'm going to get you a bottle of water and something to eat," they decided abruptly, and pointed a finger at her. "Stay here."

"I've got it, Kody," a new voice said, and Rebecca jolted again as Cade stepped up beside them.

"Here you go, little one." He handed Rebecca an open bottle of water and a small plate with a handful of almonds, a square of chocolate, and several slices of cheese.

If anyone had asked, she would have said she wasn't thirsty or hungry, but she had to force herself not to snatch the items out of Cade's hands. "Thank you, Sir," she said, and took a deep drink.

"Eat the food, too," he urged, and turned to Kody. "Nick sent me over to check on her."

Kody nodded. "Good enough. Thanks for the spanks, Becca."

Mouth full, Rebecca could only smile and nod, and Kody shot her a smile and a wink before fading back into the crowd.

Cade nodded at the plate in her hand. "Every bit of it," he told her, then turned to smile at Sadie. "Sadie, my favorite brat. You're looking festive."

"Thank you, Sir," Sadie replied, and with a dimple-popping grin, got up to turn in a wobbly circle. "I bought it specially."

"So I see," Cade replied with a grin of his own, and Rebecca took advantage of his preoccupation to study him.

He was shorter than Nick, a little under six feet, and dressed in a pair of trim slacks and a green dress shirt that set off both his muscled physique and his golden skin. When she'd first met him at Christmas, he'd worn his dark hair buzzed short, but it had grown since then, and curled over his ears now. His beard was the scruffy-looking kind, with the hair growing naturally up into his cheeks and down into his neck. Normally she preferred facial hair on a man to be trimmed and tidy, like Nick's, but the wild look worked on Cade, and his beard looked smooth and sleek as a mink pelt.

His deep brown eyes were surrounded by thick lashes, his smile was slow and sexy, and if she hadn't been madly in love with Nick, she would definitely have been interested.

The thought made her want to squirm in familiar discomfort. He was arguably Nick's best friend, but in the nearly three months she and Nick had been together, she'd spoken to him only a handful of times. He and Nick got together to hang out regularly, along with the rest of the guys that made up Nick's core friendship group, all of them part of the kink scene. But she'd only seen him at parties, and he'd never approached her without Nick by her side.

Which was both a relief and a disappointment, because she had a little crush on him. And while on one level she enjoyed the flutter that rose in her belly whenever he smiled at her, on another level it made her profoundly uncomfortable. Nick didn't miss much, so even though it had never come up, she was almost certain he knew about the crush. And clearly she wouldn't be acting on it, though if she were single she would certainly be tempted.

Cade was charming and clever, and by all accounts a thorough and attentive Dominant. She knew she'd enjoy playing with him, which she tried her best not to think about since she was in a committed, monogamous relationship.

But then Nick had broached the idea of teaming up with Cade to make her threesome fantasy a reality, and she'd been thinking almost nonstop ever since.

Rebecca jerked her attention back to the present just as Sadie attempted a curtsey in her very short skirt and very high heels. She wobbled, nearly tipping herself over into the unforgiving brick of the fireplace. Quick as lightning, Cade stepped forward to grab her arms.

"Maybe you should just sit," he suggested.

"No, I can do this," she declared, then bit her lip. "But maybe hold my hands?"

"Sure," he said, humor dancing in his eyes once again, and shifted his grip to her hands.

Sadie lowered herself slowly, holding on to Cade so tight her knuckles were white, then just as slowly eased back up.

"Nailed it," she crowed, still holding on to Cade. "Can you help me sit now?"

"Sure," Cade replied, and didn't let go until she was safely sitting on the hearth once again. "I can always count on you to brighten the room, Sadie."

"Aw, you're just the sweetest," Sadie purred back, fluttering her long false eyelashes—green, with sparkling gold tips—in response. "Isn't he the sweetest, Becca?"

Rebecca blinked as Cade turned to her, the humor in his eyes changing to something darker. Her high heels put her within an inch or two of his height, giving her no choice but to look him in the eye.

"I think Becca might not think me so sweet, since I'm here to add to her punishment." He lifted a dark eyebrow in question, his eyes locked on hers. His dark gaze was just as intense as Nick's crystal-blue one, she thought absently. She nearly sagged with relief when his gaze dropped to her hands. "All finished?"

She blinked at the empty plate. "Yes, Sir."

"Good. Sadie, do you think you can walk to the garbage can without falling down?""

"Sure." Sadie rose, her eyes gleaming at Rebecca as she relieved her of the plate and water bottle. "Be right back."

Rebecca watched her friend totter away, then squared her shoulders and turned back to Cade. "I'm ready, Sir."

She'd barely begun to turn when a hard hand on her elbow stopped her. Startled, she looked up at Cade. "Sir?"

"Not here," he told her, and slid his hand down her arm to grasp her hand. "Come with me."

Her throat slammed shut, panic rooting her feet to the ground. She shook her head. "Sir, I'm not supposed to leave the room."

"You're not," he assured her, his eyes steady and his voice calm. He angled his head, nodding at something or someone across the room. "I'm taking you to Nick."

"Oh." Rebecca looked up and spotted Nick leaning against one of the spanking benches that had been set up on the play side of the room. Even with the distance she could see him smile, and she relaxed. "I'm sorry, Sir."

"No worries," he replied easily, and began towing her across the room. "How are you doing?"

"Fine, Sir," she replied, the words automatic even as she winced. Her butt was sore, more so than she'd realized, and walking was uncomfortable. "Or fine enough, I guess."

His gaze flicked down to her backside and up again. "Kody caught you good."

"Right across the sit spot, both times," she said with a sigh, then glanced at him with a tentative smile when he laughed. "Y'all do love to 'same damn spot' us, don't you?"

"Sometimes," he said, shooting her a look out of unreadable eyes. "And sometimes it's fun to forge new territory."

She almost asked "Like what?" but remembered where she was—and who she was talking to—just in time. Some questions it was better not to ask.

So she made a noncommittal 'mmhmm' noise that, by the knowing smirk he shot her, didn't fool him in the slightest. But then they reached the spanking bench, and Nick, and she was saved from any further questions by the love of her life.

He stepped forward, lifting his hands to cup her face. "There's my good girl."

He tilted her face up for his kiss, soft and sweet, then pulled back to look at her. "You didn't come to get me, not even once."

She shook her head. Though there were one or two people in the room she would absolutely have refused, like Joel—there was something about that kid she just didn't like—everyone who'd approached her had followed the rules.

"How's your ass?"

"Sore, but not terrible," she answered honestly. She'd learned over the last few months that with Nick, honesty was absolutely the best policy. If she tried to downplay her level of pain because she wanted more play, or to prove her strength or resilience, he got mad at her for not taking care of herself. And if she tried to exaggerate it to end a scene faster, he got mad because she was topping from the bottom. There was no scenario in which lying to Nick served her well, so she just didn't.

"Show me," he said, and she began to turn so he could view the damage for himself. A tug on her hand made her look down, surprised to see Cade was still holding on. She looked up, her belly fluttering as she realized he was watching her with an odd light in his eyes. Then he dropped her hand, and she turned to show Nick her butt.

"Hmm." He skimmed rough fingers over her sensitized skin, and her breath hitched. "Red, maybe lightly bruised. Doesn't look like anyone went too hard on you, love."

She shook her head. "No, Daddy."

"Who hit you the hardest with their bare hand?"

His fingers were still tracing the marks on her skin, distracting and arousing, and she had to force herself to concentrate. "James."

"And who hit you the hardest with something else?"

"Kody," she replied. "I think."

His hand stilled on her butt. "You think?"

She glanced at him over her shoulder. "I'm pretty sure, but they hit me last, so it could be that it's just the freshest."

"Ah." His hand dropped lower, brushing against the red marks on the crease between thigh and buttock. "This is Kody's?"

"Yes."

"I can barely tell where the marks overlap," Nick mused, and glanced at Cade. "They're getting better with that paddle."

Cade grinned. "You should've seen the look on their face when they wound up. Kid in a candy store."

Nick barked out a laugh. "Nice. Well, I'd say you took your punishment very well, Rebecca."

She turned around to face him again with a sigh of relief. "Thank you, Daddy."

"Tell me how you felt."

It wasn't an unexpected question. Though they'd known each other for years, they'd only been romantically involved for a few months, and they were still getting to know each other as Dominant and submissive. He could probably make an accurate guess as to how a given activity or punishment—or, in this case, funishment—would make her feel, but he also wanted her to evaluate and articulate her feelings.

"Uncomfortable," she admitted. "I don't like being the center of attention."

"I know."

She fought not to squirm as she continued. "It was worse when James did it, because everyone was watching. I couldn't pretend they weren't."

He nodded, his eyes calm. She took a steadying breath and went on. "It was better after that. Not great, because I couldn't really relax thinking any minute someone was going to come up and demand their two smacks, but…it was better."

"Did worrying about it make it better or worse?"

She sighed, knowing where this was going. "Worse. It made it worse."

"All right, then," he said, apparently willing to let the point go unsaid for now. "Ready for the next part of your punishment?"

Shit. She'd forgotten there was a part two. She started to nod, then paused, brow furrowing as she turned to Cade. "I thought…"

"Oh, I'm not spanking you," he said easily, his lips curving.

"But you said—"

"That I was going to add to your punishment," he reminded her. "And I am."

"I asked Cade to help me with part two," Nick interjected smoothly as Cade crouched to unzip the black bag at the base of the spanking bench. "He's better with rope than I am."

Rebecca blinked. "Rope?"

"Rope," Nick confirmed, and turned to Cade. "What's first?"

"Get her out of those shoes," Cade said, his head still bent over the duffel bag. He was pulling out bundles of rope dyed a pretty green, stacking them one on top of the other. He flicked a glance up and over her, coolly assessing. "I need her hair out of the way, too."

"You got it," Nick said, and crouched to tap her foot. "Lift up your foot, baby girl, so I can get this off."

Rebecca stared at the growing pile of rope as she obeyed, lifting first one foot, then the other, her hand on Nick's shoulder for balance. When her shoes were off, he set them aside and rose, pulling an elastic out of his pocket. He moved behind her and began gathering her hair.

"Nick?" she said, her voice high and shaky with nerves.

"Who?" he asked almost absently.

She licked her lips. "Daddy," she amended. "What's going on?"

"This is part two of your punishment," he explained as he swiftly wove her hair into a simple braid that hung down her back. He moved to stand in front of her and tugged the green ribbon from her hair, then pulled her braid over her shoulder and tied a bow on the end of it.

She eyed the pile of rope at Cade's feet with dread. It was a lot of fucking rope, more than would be needed to tie her hands and feet. "Are you going to tie me to something?"

"I'm not tying you at all," he informed her, and stepped to the side. "How's that?"

How's what? she almost asked, then jolted when Cade said, "I can work with that," and she realized he hadn't been asking her.

Chapter Seven

All the spit in Rebecca's mouth dried up as Cade stepped forward, a length of rope in his hands and his dark, heavy eyes on hers. "How experienced are you at rope bondage, pretty girl?"

"Um." She had to swallow twice to make her voice work, her eyes locked on the rope in his hands. "I've been tied up a few times, Sir."

"Ever had this much rope on you?" he asked, indicating the pile at their feet.

She shook her head. 'No, Sir. Mostly just hands and feet."

"All right. I need you to stand still while I work, and keep your knees bent," he told her. "I also need you to tell me if anything pinches or drags at your skin, understand?"

"Yes," she whispered, her gaze shifting from the rope, to Cade's face, to Nick's. "Yes, I understand."

"Good. Do you need to hit the bathroom before we begin?"

She hesitated for a moment, the temptation to lie great. If she could just hide in the bathroom for a few minutes, get her bearings…

She shook her head. "No, Sir. I'm fine."

"All right, then." He gave her a small smile that might have been reassuring but for the devilish twinkle in his eye, and circled to stand behind her. "Lift your arms for me, put your hands on your head."

She did as she was told, her gaze locked on Nick he came to stand in front of her. She sucked in a sharp breath when Cade reached around her body, his hands warm and hard on her skin as he wrapped the rope around her, just above her breasts.

"Breathe, Rebecca," Nick murmured, and she let out the breath she'd been holding and sucked in another one. "There we go. You're such a good girl, Rebecca. Such a good girl, and I love you so much."

She clung to the words, keeping her eyes locked on his as Cade continued to wind the rope around her. She tried to lose herself in them, to drown in their icy blue depths, but as much as she tried to block it out, she was acutely aware of every move Cade made. She felt every slither of rope over her skin, every brush of his hands on her breasts, on her back. Everywhere he touched seemed to crackle with electricity, her skin all but buzzing with it.

"You're doing so well," Nick told her, his voice both a comfort and a tease. She could see by the look in his eyes that he knew what she was feeling, how aroused and needy her body was becoming, but he made no move to ease her ache.

And the rope, oh, the rope. It was like another pair of hands, squeezing and holding her, a torment all its own.

He wound it around her torso, above and below her breasts, snug but not too tight. It hugged her harder with each inhale, but didn't constrict her breathing. He ran it around the back of her neck and down between her breasts, creating a basic chest harness. She gazed down at her chest as he worked, the green rope bright against her skin. She'd never done any decorative bondage like this, and she was surprised at both how pretty it was and how amazing it felt. Her breasts were lightly compressed by the bands of rope, making them swell and ache. She'd already spent a couple of hours in acute arousal, and the gentle compression of her breasts was an added layer of sensation.

"Shit, you look good," Nick said, jerking her attention back to him.

In the last few months she'd seen Nick aroused plenty of times, but she'd never seen him like this. There was fire in his eyes, and a feral kind of lust that made her tremble in anticipation. She didn't have to look at his crotch to know he was hard and ready, and she knew under different circumstances he'd already have her bent over and filled with his straining cock.

But Nick was nothing if not disciplined, and not even his own need was going to distract him from whatever he had planned.

As if to underscore the point, Cade stood in front of her again, another length of rope in his hands. "Doing all right, Becca?"

She nodded, looking up at him now that she was barefoot. He really was so handsome. His dark hair and eyes were the opposite of Nick's blond and blue, but no less impactful. His good looks alone were enough to make her belly clutch, but the way he watched her was the icing on the perverted cake.

He watched her like she was prey, and she liked it.

"Good," he said, and reached around her, rope in hand. "Keep your hands up and out of the way, menina."

Menina? She frowned over the unfamiliar word, and opened her mouth to ask about it. Then she shut it again, unsure of the protocol expected of her.

He glanced at her face, a faint smile curling his mouth. He must have seen the question in her eyes, because he said, "It means 'girl' in Portuguese."

"Oh." She had more questions, like how and why he'd learned to speak Portuguese, but when he made no effort to explain further, she stayed silent.

Her body jerked and swayed as he wrapped rope around her torso again and again, pushing the ends through the previous pass to create a corset that extended from just below her breasts to the top of her hips. It was snug, and her breathing was a little more constricted now, every breath pulling it tighter in a rough caress.

"Take a couple of deep breaths for me, Becca," Cade demanded, and she obeyed, her ribcage expanding as she filled her lungs, forcing her skin hard against the rope. He made her do it twice more, reaching out to make small adjustments, then nodded in satisfaction and turned to Nick.

"Go ahead and do your thing while I get the next rope ready."

Rebecca's gaze darted to Nick as he stepped forward, guilt an uncomfortable twinge in her chest. She'd been so distracted by Cade, and the rope, and in trying to control her body's reaction to both that she'd forgotten he was there for a moment.

Laughter lurked in his beautiful eyes. "Forgot I was here, didn't you?"

"In my defense, getting tied up is pretty distracting."

"Oh, I'm sure."

She winced. "Are you mad?"

"No, beautiful." He lifted his hand to cup her cheek, and she leaned into it, the simple caress soothing her soul. "You did exactly what I expected you to do."

"Space out?" she suggested impishly, relaxing as the guilt faded.

"Concentrate on Cade so I could get a few things out of my bag without you noticing," he replied, lust and laughter in his gleaming eyes.

She looked down quickly, but his other hand was tucked behind his back, and she couldn't see what had put that sadistic gleam in his eyes.

He tapped his fingers on her cheek firmly. Not hitting her exactly, but definitely getting her attention. Her gaze flew back to his.

"Turn around and bend over the bench," he instructed, and shifted his hand from her face to her shoulder to nudge her into obeying.

She draped herself over the hip high bench. It was narrow, barely wider than a saw horse, with ledges for knees and elbows to rest and handles for gripping. She wrapped her hands around them, forcing herself not to hold on too hard, and laid her cheek on the padded top. Her breasts dangled heavily on either side, and lying on top of the rope circling her torso added pressure where she wasn't used to having any. It was so distracting that when Nick laid a hand on her butt, she jumped in surprise.

He chuckled, rich and low. "I'm going to have to up my bondage game," he decided. "It distracts you so delightfully."

"Sorry, Daddy."

"Nothing to be sorry for, sweet girl." He stroked her tender bottom once in a rough caress, then tapped her inner thigh firmly. "Spread your legs."

She inched them apart, her hands tightening on the grips. He tapped again, and she kept moving until he stopped her. "That's good. Tilt your ass up, now, that's my pretty girl. What do you think, Cade?"

"Gorgeous," Cade replied from somewhere behind her, and the compliment made her squirm. She didn't have to look behind her to know they were both looking at her exposed genitals—she could all but feel the weight of their eyes on her, and her already wet pussy grew even wetter.

"I'm just about ready, here," Cade announced.

"Then I guess I better get this show on the road."

There was a quiet click, then the cool trickle of lube over her exposed anus. It wasn't entirely unexpected—Nick rarely passed up an opportunity to put something in her ass—but she was on edge and the lube was cold, so she flinched.

"It'll warm up soon," Nick assured her with a chuckle. He added another squirt of lube, then something firm pressed against her. "Deep breath, love."

She obeyed, her breath hitching as the object breached the sensitive opening. It was cold, colder than the lube, and hard. Metal, she realized. She didn't own a metal plug, and neither did Nick as far as she knew. If he did, he'd surely have brought it out before now.

It must be new, she thought, but then he pushed harder and every coherent thought fled.

Pain burned bright as her asshole stretched to accommodate it. The tip was big, bigger than she was used to, and she knew from experience that it would get worse before it got better. She sucked in a breath and tried to relax, bracing herself for more pain, then suddenly it was gone.

She blinked, startled by the sudden absence of pain, and gave an experimental wiggle. There was definitely something inside her—there was pressure and weight and the full feeling of penetration—but her anus was no longer spread wide, and there was something lying against her tailbone.

She craned her neck around, trying to see what it was, and saw the glint of steel resting there. "What…?"

"Ass hook," Nick told her, and tapped the metal so it shifted ever so slightly inside her. "There's a one-inch ball on the other end. How does it feel?"

"Different," she managed. "Full, but not like a plug."

"Good?" he asked.

"I'm not sure."

"Fair enough. Try to stand up."

She carefully pushed up off the bench. The hook shifted inside her, sliding and rubbing against the sensitive inner channel, slick with lube and remarkably heavy. She moved slowly, clenching her anus to keep it in place as she turned.

"Relax," Nick said, rubbing her arms. "It won't fall out."

"It's heavy," she told him.

"I know." Some of his earlier delight came back into his eyes. "But the angle of the hook will keep it in place. So will the rope."

"The rope?" She frowned. How could the rope keep it in place?

"The rope," Cade confirmed, and moved behind her.

She squeaked when he tugged on the hook, her eyes wide on Nick's. "What's he doing?"

"There's a hole in the end of it for tying it in place," he told her, gripping her shoulders now to keep her in place.

"I'm anchoring it to the chest harness," Cade said, and right on cue the ropes above and below her breasts tightened as he pulled on them. "I thought about tying it to your hands, but Nick doesn't want them bound."

"Well." Nick sent her a wink. "Not like that, anyway."

"And this way," Cade went on, pulling up on the hook so she rose to her toes with a squeak, "I can put it where I want it, and you can't change the tension by moving your arms."

"She still has to be able to walk," Nick reminded him.

"Not as much fun, but okay." The tension eased a fraction. "Better?"

Nick's gaze flicked to her feet, flat on the ground once more. "That should be good."

There was a series of tugs as Cade tied off the rope, each one jerking the hook. The pressure was surprisingly intense, the steel ball heavy inside her. Her arousal was reaching the point that she began to drift, so when Cade crouched in front of her, she simply stared down at him in confusion. "What?"

His grin was lightning quick and completely evil. "I said, spread your legs."

"Oh. Sorry." She stepped her feet apart, careful to keep her knees relaxed. "How's that?"

"Perfect. Now put your hands flat on your thighs. Just like that, darlin'. Now hold still for me."

"'Kay," she murmured.

"Look at me, Rebecca," Nick said, and she looked up. Nick was smiling down at her, amusement and concern in his pretty eyes.

"Hi, Daddy," she said, swaying toward him.

"Hi." Nick glanced down at Cade, who was winding more rope around her thighs, binding her hands to her legs. It felt rough and warm and delicious, and she wiggled with pleasure. "I think she's rope drunk."

Cade snorted out a laugh. "I better hurry or she's going to be done before you even get started."

"Best laid plans," Nick said with a sigh, but he was smiling.

She could feel her heartbeat in her clit, and desire flowed through her like honey, slow and thick. She felt drugged, like her body had been taken over by lazy pleasure, and trying to move was like pushing through warm mud.

It felt amazing, and she might have been content so stay there, swimming through the heavy heat and pulse of her own blood, if she hadn't been so damn turned on.

She blinked up at her lover, watching her so closely, so carefully. "Daddy?"

His thumb moved across her cheek in a gentle caress. "Yes, love?"

She licked her lips, shuddering when his eyes tracked the movement. "I'm horny."

"I know," he said over Cade's snort. "I can smell you."

She blushed, shame and arousal staining her cheeks pink. Then he leaned forward and whispered, "And so can Cade."

She shook her head. *No, he can't. Can he?*

Nick smirked and angled her chin so she was looking down at Cade, crouched between them and winding rope around her left thigh.

He looked up, his face mere inches away from the tangled thatch of pubic hair decorating her mound, and winked. "Smells like sweet candy pussy," he said, and her face simply went up in flames.

Oh, God.

"Sweetest I've ever had," Nick said easily, like he was talking about the weather or the Cardinals' chances for the World Series this year instead of *how her pussy tasted.*

"Wouldn't mind trying that sometime," Cade replied, his head bent once again to his task, seemingly oblivious to the fact that Rebecca was half a breath away from either spontaneously exploding into orgasm or a heart attack. She figured it could go either way.

The scales tipped toward orgasm when Nick slid his hand between her legs.

"Oh, yeah," he said, his voice faint through the sudden roaring in her ears as he skimmed his fingers, whisper light, through the dripping folds between her thighs. God, she'd been on edge for *hours* now, aching for his touch, and now that she was finally getting it, it wasn't nearly enough.

"Stand still," he warned, and she gritted her teeth. She hadn't even moved yet, but of course he knew she wanted to. She just needed a little more pressure and friction in the right spot and she could come. Hell, she was so primed for orgasm that a little more pressure and friction in the *wrong* spot just might do it. But she could tell by the gleam in his eye he wasn't going to give it to her.

"Ready here," Cade said, and Nick pulled his hand away. Her whimper of protest earned her a wolfish grin. She might have tried to glare at him—if she could manage it, her mind felt so scattered she wasn't at all sure she could pull it off—but then Cade reached between her legs and what was left of her coherent thoughts scattered to the winds.

Her legs were still parted, so he had no trouble getting between them. She jerked her hands forward in an instinctive attempt to cover herself, but they didn't move, and when she looked down, she realized he'd secured her hands to her thighs when she hadn't been paying attention.

Helpless, with no way to stop him short of using her safeword, she watched him run a thick length of rope between his hands. The slight tug on the ropes around her waist told her he'd attached the new one to them, and now he was pulling it forward between her splayed, wet thighs.

He held it up to the rope crossing her belly, eyed it as though he were measuring it, then tied a knot in it. She frowned, not understanding what was happening—why was he tying a knot where it wouldn't attach to anything?—then he looped the ends though the ropes at her stomach and pulled, and she clued in.

The knot rested just below her pubic hair, tucked in the space between her clit and her mound, and when he cinched it tight it put a hard, unyielding pressure in almost exactly the right spot.

"Not too tight, right?" Cade asked.

"Yeah, I don't want her getting off," Nick replied.

Cade gave it some slack, swiftly tied the ends to the ropes encircling her waist, then sat back on his heels. "Check that and tell me what you think."

Nick reached between her thighs once again, his fingertips tracing the rope between them. *Ropes*, she amended. There were two of them, the strands spread on either side of her labia before coming together in the knot near her clit.

"She's got thick labia," Cade said, "so I think the rope will stay put at that tension. But even if it slips down, it won't cause too much damage. A little chafing, that's all."

"Good," Nick said while Rebecca thought, *A little chafing?* "Rebecca, how does it feel?"

She licked her lips. "Strange. The knot..."

"Fun, isn't it?" he said with a grin, and tapped the knot so firmly that her knees almost buckled.

Cade's low laugh matched Nick's. "I think she likes it."

She honestly didn't know if she liked it or not, she just knew she needed to come. "Please, Daddy?"

"Please what?" he asked absently, his fingers still playing between her legs.

"I need to come."

"No." He raised a stern eyebrow when her jaw dropped. "I feel like you've forgotten something, baby girl. This is supposed to be a punishment."

He pulled his hand away and, ignoring her whimper of protest, lifted it to the light. His fingertips were wet, gleaming with the evidence of her arousal. "So, the answer is no. You don't get to come tonight."

It took her a full five seconds to find her voice. "At all?"

"At all," he confirmed, and reached out to trace his fingertips over her mouth, transferring the juices from one set of lips to the other. He chuckled when her gaze darted to the front of his jeans, where it was obvious he was every bit as turned on as she was. "Oh, I'll be coming. But you won't."

Oh, he was *diabolical*. She wasn't sure if she wanted to punch him in the face or fall sobbing to her knees. Thanks to her bound hands she couldn't do the first, and if she did the second, she'd probably fall on her face and break her nose.

"She's pretty when she's pissed off, isn't she?" Nick asked Cade, who'd risen to his feet so the two men stood shoulder to shoulder, identical smug expressions on their ridiculously handsome faces, and now she wanted to hit both of them.

"Gorgeous," Cade agreed, stepping in front of her. His eyes were locked on her mouth, and she had one moment to wonder what the heck he was doing. Then he bent his head and very softly, very delicately, licked her lips.

Rebecca inhaled sharply, frozen to the spot. It wasn't a kiss, not really. He didn't press his lips to hers or attempt to force them apart. He just slicked his tongue over her mouth, first the bottom lip then the top, scooping up the wetness Nick had left behind.

When he was finished, he eased back, licking his lips as though he was savoring a particularly tasty snack, and said, "I was right. Sweet candy pussy."

She stood there in the thrumming silence, her mind a muddle and her body hot and heavy, until Nick clapped a hand on Cade's shoulder and broke the spell.

"Thanks for the help."

"Anytime." Cade stepped back, his gaze falling away from Rebecca's as he bent to pick up his bag. "I'll catch up with you later."

Nick nodded as Cade strolled away, and stepped up to Rebecca. "Give me a color, sweetheart."

"Um." She swallowed and forced herself to think. The bondage was confining and unfamiliar, but it wasn't putting undue strain on her muscles or causing her any pain. And while she was very, very confused about what had just happened, she wasn't upset by it. Just the opposite, in fact.

"Green," she finally said. "And confused."

His lips twitched behind his beard. "What are you confused about, love?"

"Um. Everything?"

"All right, then, I'll see if I can explain everything." He picked up her braid and dropped it behind her shoulder to hang down her back. "First, you don't get to come because you came without permission the other night. It seemed fitting that the punishment for that would be fewer orgasms, not more."

She had to admit it made perfectly logical sense, so she nodded, even though her pussy wasn't in the mood to be logical.

"And I asked Cade to help me with the bondage because I'm out of practice." He dropped his gaze and skimmed his hands down her breasts to her waist, circled by yards of green rope. "Though I may have to pick it up again, because I'm seriously loving how this looks on you. I may have to get some pictures before we untie you."

Pictures. The idea made her want to both cringe and preen. She'd never thought about doing a fetish shoot, or having any kind of intimate photographs taken, but the look in Nick's eye made her want to consider it. His birthday was coming up in a few months, and had been wondering what to get him…

"Any other questions?"

She blinked back to the present. "Why did he kiss me?"

"Did you like him kissing you?"

She opened her mouth to answer, then closed it again. It felt like a trick question, and she wasn't sure how to answer it.

"It's not a trick question," Nick went on, reading her mind as usual. "There's no wrong answer. If you didn't like it, he won't ever do it again."

She licked her lips, tasting the faint remains of her own arousal and a hint of mint that could only have come from Cade. *Oh, God.* "And if I did?"

"Then we'll have to talk about whether you want him to do it again."

"I liked it," she confessed, her cheeks heating at the admission.

"There's my honest girl," he said softly, and laid his lips gently on hers. She tried to take the kiss deeper, and he pulled back with a chuckle. "None of that, now."

"Are you really going to torture me all night?"

"I really am," he said with unmistakable glee, and stepped back. "Now, let me see how you walk in all that."

She bit back a pout—it wouldn't do her any good, and might get her into even more trouble—and took a tentative step forward. It was odd, not being able to use her arms for balance, and the rope bit into her skin a bit as her thighs flexed, but it wasn't terrible.

No, what was terrible was the rope running between her legs. With every step, the lightly abrasive hemp scraped along the delicate lips of her pussy, and the knot bumped into her clit. And oh, her ass. She'd forgotten about the hook, her body having adapted to it, but the minute she moved the pressure and fullness came rushing back. It all felt amazing, but it wasn't nearly enough to get her off.

"How's it feel?" he asked, and she raised stricken eyes to his.

"That bad, huh?" he asked, clearly delighted.

"You are so mean to me," she said, only half joking.

"You love it," he told her, and she didn't have a counter argument because yes, she loved it, but oh my *God,* she was going to *die.*

"Come on," he said, draping an arm around her shoulders. "Let's go take a walk around the room."

"Like this?" she asked automatically, some of her outrage leaking through.

"I can add an egg vibrator, if you're complaining," he said, his tone leaving no doubt that he was completely serious.

"Not complaining," she said, not wanting that at all. He liked to use the lowest setting, ensuring that her arousal stayed high and the chances of her coming low, a habit that should've given her a clue that something like this was on the horizon.

"Then let's go see what our friends are up to this evening," he said, and pulled her across the room.

Chapter Eight

Rebecca was just about at the end of her rope—so to speak—and Nick wasn't far behind.

It had been about an hour since Cade had finished tying her up, and in that time they'd made two slow circuits of the basement. They'd stopped to chat with friends, paused to observe scenes in progress, taken one quick bathroom break—and that had been interesting—and he figured he'd pushed her just about as far as he could.

Her face and chest were flushed, her nipples were so hard they could cut glass, and her whole body trembled every time she moved. Her skin glowed with a fine sheen of sweat, the edges of her scalp damp with it, and though she was still alert enough to walk without help and participate in conversation, her normally smooth movements had turned awkward, and her voice was so soaked in need and desperation that every word sounded like a plea for mercy.

He'd bet his car that she was so painfully aroused she was verging on desperate, and if that hadn't been his exact goal, he might have felt pity.

He knew he had to get her out of the bondage soon. He'd caught Cade's eye from across the room a few minutes ago, and the signal that his time was just about up. He'd been debating with himself about whether or not to cut her loose before he could implement the last part of his plan, and figured if he wanted to keep her tied up for the grand finale, he was going to have to get to it.

They were watching a scene in the main bedroom, a threesome scene between two men and one woman. He'd thought to gauge her interest in it, to see if she found the visual arousing. But while she was staring at the trio on the bed as though riveted, it was clear the state of her own body held much of her attention.

He wrapped a hand around the length of metal protruding from her ass and waited for her instinctive jolt. The first time he'd grabbed on to it to direct her to move he hadn't waited, and the movement of the steel ball inside her had nearly sent her over the edge. He didn't want that to happen—having to devise a punishment for coming without permission *while being punished for coming without permission* wasn't something he wanted to spend his time on tonight. Thank God she'd managed to hold off, and now he was much more careful with how he grabbed that hook.

Although it was big fun, and he made a mental note to ask Cade if he could buy it from him.

"Come with me," he murmured in her ear, his voice low so as not to interrupt the scene, and steered her toward the door. She went willingly, her steps not nearly as graceful as they'd been an hour ago.

He caught Cade's eye again as they strolled through the main room, and mouthed "Five minutes." Cade's gaze flicked to Rebecca, assessing, then nodded in agreement.

Nick steered Rebecca to the small alcove next to the powder room under the stairs. It wasn't really a room, just a bit of space that didn't have any other function, but it was out of the way and big enough for his purposes, and that was all he cared about.

He steered her to the back corner, making sure anyone who needed the powder room could get around them, then stopped. She looked up at him with those big, soft eyes, so needy she was begging him without saying a word. She didn't even spare a glance for where they were, or show any hint of confusion about why they were there. She was focused entirely on him, utterly subservient as she waited for him to tell her what to do, and it was hot as fuck.

"On your knees," he said, his voice rough with need, and he half pushed, half helped her lower down. She stayed in the kneel-up position, whether because she knew what he was about to do or because sitting back on her heels would've put unbearable pressure on the hook and the rope, he didn't know. And he didn't care.

He was already tearing at his fly, grunting when his cock bounced free. He was so hard it was standing nearly straight up, the head already slick.

He grabbed the base in one hand, wrapped the other around the back of her head, and dragged her forward. "Suck."

Her mouth was already open, eyes shining as she took him in. "Yes, baby, just like that. Suck Daddy's cock."

He let go of his dick to grab her head in both hands. She opened her mouth wider, flattening her tongue against the bottom of his shaft and sticking it out, an unspoken invitation for more, and with a growl he let loose.

He pushed steadily in, not stopping when he hit the back of her throat. Her muscles rippled around him, the convulsive flex of her throat trying to block or accommodate the intruder. He pushed past it, his eyes locked on her face as he tunneled deep into her throat. Her eyes watered, tears slipping down her cheeks.

"That's my good girl," he rasped, pulling back slightly to let her get a breath before pushing in again. "That's it, take all of me. Take Daddy deep, show me how much you want it."

He knew he wouldn't last long—his balls were already tight against the base of his shaft, sensation crawling through his belly as the orgasm approached. But the warm, wet cavern of her mouth felt like heaven, the stroke of her tongue a carnal delight, and if he couldn't make it last, then at least he could enjoy to the fullest.

He picked up speed, shoving his cock into her throat over and over again. Spit flew, dripping down her chin and spattering on his pants, and the wet, gurling sound of his cock hitting her throat was music to his deviant ears.

"That's my girl," he ground out, giving her the dirty talk she loved. "That's Daddy's little slut. You going to swallow my load like a good little fucktoy?"

She gurgled her answer, her eyes streaming. She fought to maintain eye contact though the hammering thrusts, her head jerking back and forth with the impact despite his fist in her hair. Spit dripped off her chin, gleamed on the taut slopes of her breasts, still confined in the ropes. He already knew he was buying some of that rope from Cade—there was no way the one between her thighs wasn't saturated by now—but at this rate they'd have bodily fluids over the rest of it, too.

And speaking of bodily fluids…

He slowed his thrusts. He knew he didn't have long before his orgasm became inevitable, but he wanted to draw it out a little bit more. He held himself deep in her mouth, her nose buried in his open fly.

"I'm going to come in your mouth," he told her, grinding the words out. "And you're going to swallow every fucking drop.

She coughed, her throat spasming on the head of his dick as she fought to control her gag reflex. He used his grip on her head to drag her back just far enough for her to suck in a deep breath, then he buried her face in his crotch again.

"Every fucking drop," he repeated, jerking her mouth on his cock like it was his fist, short little thrusts that kept him buried deep. "If you spit it out, if you miss a single drop, I swear you won't come for a month."

Her eyes went wide at the threat, and he grinned. He wouldn't follow through on it—it was pure bluff, the kind of in-scene dirty talk that made both of them hotter. But she didn't know that, and she was so on edge from not being allowed to orgasm all night that she would likely do anything to keep from prolonging the agony.

"Fuck, here it comes." He dragged her back and forth on his cock once, twice, then shoved himself deep and held her tight as the orgasm exploded out of him.

She took the first shots right down her gullet, her throat massaging his cock, and the pleasure nearly buckled his knees. He pulled back slightly so she could taste the next one, jerking the base of his cock as he flooded her mouth. She sucked hard, her cheeks hollowing as she worked her tongue around him, swallowing fast to keep up.

When he was drained, and she'd lapped up every drop, he eased his cock from her lips. "Good girl," he rasped, quickly tucking himself away. She swayed on her knees in front of him, her makeup streaking her face and drool dripping from her chin. Her eyes were glassy and her cheeks were flushed, her body racked by shivers.

"Can I come now, Daddy?" she asked, her voice ragged and desperate.

"No, baby, not tonight," he said, steeling himself as her eyes welled with tears of frustration. Part of him hated to deprive her, especially in this state. But he needed to follow the rules he'd set, and knowing she'd take what he gave her—even when it hurt—was a satisfaction that rivaled even the best orgasm.

He helped her to her feet, holding her up when her knees threatened to buckle, and looked around for Cade. He was standing ten feet away, and hurried over at Nick's nod. He moved directly behind Rebecca and began working at the knots in the rope.

"Hold on, sweetheart." He kept one hand on her face, the other on her hip, and tried to stay out of Cade's way. "Cade will have you free in just a minute, then we'll go home, all right?"

"It hurts," she choked out, her face buried in his throat.

"What hurts, baby?" he asked. Cade worked faster, his fingers flying through the knots and dropping the ropes in a tangled pile at their feet.

"I need to come so badly," she whispered, and the agony in her voice twisted in his gut even as his dick began to harden again.

"I know, baby." He pressed his lips to her forehead, holding her close as she trembled and shook. Absorbing her pain, even as he refused to assuage it. Her hands, newly freed, dug into his shirt. "I'm sorry that you can't."

"Almost done," Cade told him, on his feet now, unwinding the yards of rope around her torso. "Chest harness and hook next."

Nick nodded, knowing what Cade wasn't saying. When the chest harness was removed, and the blood that had been restricted began to flow through her breasts again, there would be a moment of relief followed by a deep, stinging pain. Under normal circumstances she'd be expecting it, he was sure. But the state she was in now—desperate, her mind fogged with pain and lust—he doubted she was aware of anything but the clamoring need within her own body.

"Can you get it off like this?" Nick asked, indicating with a jerk of his head the way she was plastered against him.

"Might be some rope burn," Cade warned.

He didn't want that. "Undo the knot, and I'll turn her around."

Cade nodded. "I'll tell you when."

Nick slid an arm around her newly bared waist, his palm grazing the deep dents the rope had left in her skin. He wanted to look at them, trace them with fingers and lips, but it would have to wait.

He held her tightly against him as Cade worked, then, at his nod, turned her in his arms. She clung to him, gripping his shirt like a lifeline, and he had to tell her three times to let go before she complied.

With some space between them the ropes loosened and fell away, and Cade worked quickly to get them off completely. Rebecca sagged against him, relief heavy in the breath that sighed out of her, and he tightened his arm around her waist a split second before she went stone rigid with pain.

"I've got you," he murmured in her ear, and shifted his grip to her tits.

She let out a short, agonized scream that he ignored, massaging her breasts hard, ruthlessly forcing her through the pain of equalization. When she slumped against him, sweaty and crying softly, he bent to press his lips to her tear-stained cheek. "I've got you."

"Hook," Cade said, pulling Nick's attention away from the trembling submissive in his arms. "Do you want to do it or should I?"

Nick hesitated. Normally he'd want to be the one to perform such an intimate act. He put it there, it was only right that he take it out. But he'd have to let go of her to do it, and he didn't know if she'd be able to stay on her feet without support.

"Let me turn her to the side," he told his friend. "Then you can do it."

Cade's surprise showed only in the slight flare in his eyes, and he nodded. "I'll hold her, if you want."

He appreciated the offer, but… "Let's do it this way."

He bent to Rebecca, speaking softly in her ear as he shifted her to stand with her shoulder against his chest. How proud he was of her, how beautiful she was, that it was almost over. He urged her to lean forward over his arm, holding her steady when she wobbled. She was almost a dead weight, leaning so heavily on his forearm that he had to brace his legs farther apart to hold her up.

It wasn't enough. He was going to drop her. "Cade."

He was there in an instant, sliding his arm into place under Nick's against Rebecca's ribs, adding his considerable strength to the task. Nick laid his other hand on the small of Rebecca's back. A chill had settled over her skin in the last few moments that he didn't like, and he jerked his chin at Cade. "Go."

Cade nodded, and Nick braced himself as Cade reached for the hook.

Rebecca lifted her head, a whimper spilling from her lips as Cade began to pull the hook from her asshole.

"Almost there, baby girl," Nick murmured, stroking his hand over her back to soothe. She stiffened as the ball of steel pulled against her sphincter, then sagged, all the tension bleeding out of her as it came free.

Cade stepped back, hook in hand, and Nick moved quickly to gather her in his arms, murmuring nonsense words of comfort and praise as she trembled and shook against him. Cade appeared with a blanket, draping it over her from behind.

"I'll clean up," he said, nodding at the pile of rope at their feet, the metal hook gleaming in his hand. "It'll be ready to go when you are."

"Thanks." Nick pressed a kiss to Rebecca's cheek and tasted tears. "I don't know if I should keep her here until she's calmer, or get her home now."

Cade narrowed his eyes, assessing. "Tough call. Can't hold her and drive at the same time."

"Exactly."

"I'll drive."

"What?"

"I'll drive," Cade repeated, and, kneeling on the floor, began to gather the pile. "Get some water in her, some fast protein, then meet me at your car. I'll drive, you can hold her in the backseat."

Nick wanted to protest that it wasn't necessary, but the trembling woman in his arms had him shoving the instinctive protest aside. "Thanks."

"No problem." Cade glanced up at him as he coiled the bright green rope, fast and efficient. "You're buying this rope, by the way."

Nick huffed out a laugh and swung Rebecca up into his arms. "And the hook. I want the hook."

"I figured." Cade jerked his head toward the stairs. "Go. I'll meet you at the car in five."

Nick nodded and headed for the stairs with his precious bundle. He'd arranged for her dress to be hung in the closet with her coat, and there were water and protein bars in the car. He'd get her into her dress, her coat, then get her into the car and home.

* * * *

Rebecca woke the next morning sure of two things. First, she was never again going to come without permission. She'd safeword out of a scene before that happened, and if there had been a stack of bibles anywhere nearby, she'd have slapped her hand on them and sworn an oath on her soul.

Second, if she didn't come soon, she was going to die.

Her entire body throbbed with unfulfilled arousal. Her nipples were hard and aching, her pussy swollen and needy. Her ass was tender from the hook, but if Nick told her she could only come if he fucked her ass with nothing but spit for lube, she'd have said to hell with anal sexual health and bent right over.

She was honestly surprised she'd been able to sleep at all with this kind of need humming through her, and she'd tossed and turned fitfully for at least an hour after Nick had tucked her into bed. But exhaustion had caught up with her, and sometime after two a.m. she'd finally drifted off.

Now she lay face down in bed, sunlight streaming through the windows, and gave serious consideration to taking matters into her own hands. She would have, if he hadn't already expressly forbidden it. Hell, she was tempted to do it even with a restriction in place. But she couldn't take another night like last night, so she tucked her hands under her pillow where they wouldn't get her into trouble and tried to go back to sleep.

After a moment, she gave up and shoved the covers aside to head for the bathroom. She had to pee, and she was thirsty enough to suck down a gallon of water straight from the Mississippi. She handled her most urgent need, then drank half the liter bottle of water that Nick had left on the bathroom counter with a sticky note that read 'drink me'. She eyed the shower while she guzzled. She felt thick-headed and sticky, and a shower sounded heavenly, but she knew there was no way she'd be able to resist the hand-held shower wand if she got in there.

She left the bathroom with a sigh, intending to find Nick and beg for some relief, but the second she walked into the bedroom she was snatched from behind. Before she could scream, she found herself flat on the bed with a naked Nick on top of her.

"Good morning," he rumbled, grinning down into her startled face. Quick as a snake, he snatched her wrists and held them above her head. "How'd you sleep?"

"Horribly," she shot back, very much not in the mood to play. She was tired, hungry, and so goddamn horny she could cry, and he was *smiling at her.*

"Aw," he said without a hint of sympathy. "Were you too cold?"

"No."

"Too hot?"

"No."

"Was the bed lumpy?"

She wanted to bite his nose right off his face. "No, the bed was not lumpy." *You jackass.*

He raised an eyebrow, and she could almost believe he'd heard what she hadn't said. "Must have been that needy, desperate pussy keeping you awake, then."

Normally she'd object to the characterization of her pussy as *desperate,* but she was too far gone to care at the moment. "Yes, it was. You got me all worked up last night then just…left me hanging!"

"I know," he said smugly, and chuckled when she gritted her teeth. "It was punishment, love. What did you expect?"

"Not that," she ground out.

"Clearly." He cocked his head, his eye narrowing slightly. "What would you rather have me do?"

She opened her mouth, then snapped it closed again. She wasn't going to give him *ideas,* for God's sake.

He smirked down at her, obviously reading her mind again. "Perhaps a beating, or forced orgasms?"

Forced orgasms didn't sound much better than not being allowed to have any at all. Contrary to popular belief, it was possible to have too much of a good thing.

"Or maybe a session with the stun gun," he said, and she couldn't control her flinch. Electrical play wasn't her favorite to begin with, and the stun gun *hurt*.

"Tell me this," he drawled, pulling her attention away from her increasingly unsettling thoughts. "After last night, are you going to try much harder not to come without permission again?"

She nodded her head so hard and fast that she almost gave herself whiplash. "Yes."

"There you go, then. If it makes you feel any better, it was punishment for me, too."

She barely bit back a snort. "Right. You got off."

"I did," he said with such relish that she had to choke back a bark of laughter. "But I like when you come. Don't get me wrong, making you suffer is fun—"

She couldn't quite hold back the snort this time, but lucky for her, he was in a playful mood and just grinned.

"But making you suffer, then not being able to make you come was hard for me." His eyes softened and his mouth sobered. "I don't like punishing you at all, Rebecca, but we have to stick to the rules we've agreed on. Otherwise, it all falls apart."

She sighed, the last of her resentment fading away. "I know, Daddy. And I'm sorry. It's just… It really felt like punishment, and I wasn't ready for it."

"You were expecting a 'funishment', weren't you?"

"I think so, yeah."

"I should've been clearer about what to expect," he said, eyeing her thoughtfully. "And maybe it's not a good idea to keep punishments secret. I thought it would keep you on your toes, but if it's going to make you too anxious—"

"It didn't." She frowned. "I don't think? If my expectations had been more realistic, it probably would've been fine."

"We'll talk about it more after you've had time to process," he told her. "And when you're not so worked up."

"Worked up?"

His grin was blade sharp. "You may have calmed down a bit since last night, but that pussy is still desperate."

"I object to the term *desperate,*" she managed, trying not to arch up into him. His chest hair was tickling her sensitive nipples, and now that she wasn't busy being mad at him, it was very distracting.

And it wasn't the only thing.

His cock was heavy against her belly, thick and hard, the tip leaving tiny puddles on her skin. It made her mouth water and her pussy ache, and just like that she was a writhing bundle of frustrated need again.

"Really?" He bent his head and gave one nipple a lazy lick. "What term would you prefer?"

"Um." She struggled to gather her scattered thoughts. "How about *very good and deserving of some dick*?"

His laugh vibrated against her breast. "Very good, huh?"

"And deserving of some dick," she finished. She was starting to pant, all the unrequited lust from last night rushing forward in a wave that had she been standing, would've brought her to her knees. She was wet and eager, her body primed. "Please, Daddy?"

"Well, since you asked so nicely." He levered himself off her and smacked her thigh. "On your stomach."

She was rolling before the words had faded, her thigh stinging and her pussy weeping. She kept her arms over her head, wrapping her fingers around one of the rings embedded in the headboard.

He ran a hand down her back, fingertips tracing the faint marks left from the rope. "Next time we do bondage, I'm definitely getting pictures," he announced, and punctuated the statement with a slap on her ass. "Legs apart."

She obeyed, spreading them as wide as she could, and tilted her hips to give him a better look at her pussy. Wet and swollen, she knew it would be readily visible between her thighs.

"Greedy slut," he said, and slapped her ass again. "Reach down here and grab your ass. Open yourself up for me. That's my girl."

She complied, fingers digging in as she held herself open for his gaze, his fingers as they traced the seam of her cunt. She was open and ready, her body all but begging him to fill her.

"Please, Daddy."

"Please what, little girl?" he asked, his tone teasing, almost absent as he continued to trace her labia, inner and outer, barely dipping a finger into the open, needy hole between them.

"Please fuck me," she begged.

"You need it?" he asked.

"Yes."

"You want it?"

"Yes," she practically sobbed. "I need *you*."

The mattress bounced when he shifted, and his knees bumped against the straining muscles of her inner thighs. "Hold that ass wide," he warned her, the broad head of his cock nudging between her lips, then, with a single, almost violent thrust, buried himself deep.

It drove the breath out of her in a cry that was almost drowned out by his heartfelt groan. "Fuck yes, baby, hold that ass open for me. Hold it open so I can fuck that needy, greedy cunt."

His hips recoiled, then thrust forward again, the impact jarring and a little painful and so goddamn good she almost came right there. But the memory of last night loomed large in her mind, and she knew she couldn't go through that again.

The words were shaky and disjointed, the way he was pumping into her making it hard for her to speak clearly, but finally she managed to ask, "Daddy, can I come?"

"Yes, baby," he ground out, circling his hips as he held himself deep inside her. "Come when you want, as often as you want. Let me feel it."

He pulled back and thrust in again, heavy and hard, and that was all it took. The heat of orgasm washed through her, down her arms and legs, swirling and tightening in her center before bursting free like water under pressure. She screamed into the pillow, her cunt tightening around his driving cock, pleasure and agony twined together inside her.

He kept fucking her when she went limp under him. "Keep that fucking ass spread," he ordered, slamming into her butt and the backs of her hands so hard the slap of it echoed around the room. "I want to see that pretty little asshole. I'm going there next, baby girl, so get ready."

"Daddy," she moaned. She was spent under him, slack and limp in the aftermath of pleasure. But the words slid into her mind like smoke, igniting the fire once again.

"Yeah, you want that." The pace of his thrusts didn't abate, the bed bouncing under the force of them. "I can feel that greedy cunt getting wetter. You like Daddy in your ass, don't you?"

"Yes, Daddy," she breathed, arching into his thrusts as desire reignited. She loved him in her ass, loved the taboo of it as much as the fullness and the pain.

"Yeah, you do. Gonna fuck your ass hard, baby. You want that?"

"Yes." She bit into the pillow to keep from screaming again. "Yes."

"As soon as you come again," he promised. "Make that slutty pussy come for me again and Daddy will fuck your ass."

"Oh my God," she wailed, the words swallowed by the pillow, lost in the slap of flesh on flesh. His grunting, filthy, dirty talk washed over her, winding through her mind. It seemed to tug at her clit, her cunt, driving her higher and higher until the orgasm was inevitable.

She came so hard she thought she blacked out, fireworks going off behind her closed eyes, and when she came back to herself, he was already halfway into her ass.

"I love watching this pretty asshole stretch around my cock," he panted, nudging forward another inch. "That's it. Take all of Daddy's cock."

The burn and the stretch were huge, the pain almost enough to overwhelm the pleasure. But the pinch in her ass made her cunt clench and her clit pulse, and when he used his big hands to knock hers aside and spread her wide, she pushed back against him.

"That's it. Fuck, I'm not going to last." He sank all the way into her ass, the coarse hair at his groin and on his legs tickling her cheeks as he bottomed out inside her. He pulled back, dragging his cock against the sensitive tunnel it was encased in, then drove back in again. "You want Daddy's come, sweetheart?"

"Yes." She was nowhere near coming again, her body wrung out by the fitful night's sleep and the two orgasms she'd already had, but it almost didn't matter. She was one big raw, pulsing nerve, lost in the fog of lust, and in that moment, more than anything, she wanted his come. "Yes, I want it."

"Where?" Thrust, retreat, thrust. "Tell me where you want it."

"In my ass." She wanted it there, *craved* it. They always used condoms when they had anal sex, hygiene and health taking precedence over fantasy. And it was fine, the right thing to do. But sometimes she didn't want to pretend she could feel him shooting his load deep inside her, didn't want to imagine his come dribbling out of her gaping asshole. Sometimes, she wanted the real thing. "In my ass, Daddy, please."

"Yeah?" He pulled all the way out, leaving her hole empty and wanting. Then he pushed in again, stretching those delicate tissues anew and driving deep. "You want Daddy to give you an anal creampie?"

The image alone almost got her there. "Oh, please."

"Hold that ass open," he ordered, and she scrabbled to put her hands back on her ass. "That's it, just like that. Hold it open for Daddy."

He pulled out again, and cold air washed over her exposed and open anus. The muscle flexed, pulling as it tried to return to its normal size, and the answering pull deep in her cunt made her moan.

"Look at that," he rasped behind her, the snap of latex as he stripped off the condom punctuating the words. "That pretty little asshole is wide open and waiting for me, isn't it?"

She flinched when he spat on her, shuddering as the warm, slick spit dribbled down the crease of her ass to slide inside her opened hole. They never used spit for the same reason they always used condoms, and also because it was a terrible lubricant.

But God, it was hot.

"You want it in your asshole, little girl?"

She nodded, twisting to look over her shoulder as best she could. He knelt on the mattress behind her, his fist working his big cock, shiny with lube. He was working the head hard, ignoring the shaft while his other hand tugged at his balls, and his eyes were narrowed on her ass. She dug her fingers in, pulling her cheeks wider and boosting her hips up just a little bit. "Please, Daddy."

His eyes darted to her face, and he leaned forward. She fought not to tense at the press of his cock, slick and hard and warm, against her puckered hole. It had closed a little, so he had to force it open again, and he moved fast, giving her no time to adjust to the burn and the stretch. She moaned again as her cunt pulsed hard in response.

"Fuck, you feel good." He fucked her shallowly, keeping himself right at the edge of her anus, the pressure on the delicate opening enormous. His thrusts became erratic, frantic. "Coming in your ass, baby girl. Take it."

He swelled inside her, stretching her impossibly wide, his shaft jerking and twitching as he pumped his load into her. Warm come flooded her rectum as he continued to move, the wet slap of his cock inside her punctuated by his grunts and groans and dirty, filthy words.

"That's Daddy's little creampie slut," he said softly, jerking the last of his come inside her. It seeped out of her, forced out by his pumping cock to froth around him where they were joined. "That's my good girl."

"I love you," she managed, her fingers still dug into her ass, keeping it spread for him. "I love you."

"My beautiful girl," he murmured. "I love you, too."

He brushed a kiss over her shoulder, his beard soft against her skin. "Keep that ass spread, now," he warned, his body tensing against hers. She nodded her agreement and he pulled out slowly, dragging his softer but still thick cock through the tenderized hole until it popped free.

"Fuck, you look good with my come leaking out of your ass," he said, and the warm trickle of it became a flood, oozing out of her opened anus. He helped her turn over, pushing and tugging at her until she was flat on her back, blinking up at him in a lust-filled haze.

"Legs up," he told her, shoving her knees back so they rested on her breasts and her ass was pointed at the ceiling. Her anus was still oozing come, trickling down her tailbone to drip on the bed, and she wondered faintly how much laundry she was going to have to do today.

"So fucking filthy," he told her, and shoved two fingers unceremoniously into her cunt. Her pussy clenched down, and he laughed. "And so fucking slutty. You want more?"

She licked her lips, uncertain how to answer that. Did she want to come again? She really did, but she wasn't sure she could handle whatever evil thought was lurking behind those crystal blue eyes.

"Yeah, you do," he said, taking her silence for an answer, and curled his fingers forward to scrape against the sensitive front wall of her pussy. "Might want to hang on to something," he suggested, and lowered his mouth to her clit.

Chapter Nine

An hour later, after two more orgasms and a shower, Rebecca finally got to eat.

"If I'd known you were this hungry, I'd have fed you before I fucked you," Nick commented mildly, watching her plow through a bacon cheeseburger and a pile of onion rings.

She snorted and picked up her milkshake. "No, you wouldn't have."

"Probably not," he agreed with a grin, and dipped a French fry in the pile of ketchup on his plate. "Do you want to talk about last night?"

She frowned. "The punishment, you mean?"

"That, or anything else."

"The punishment…I get why you did it that way. If you'd let me come, it probably would've felt like a regular scene, you know? But since you didn't…"

"A very effective punishment, I'd say," he said, and she had to agree.

"I didn't like it, but yeah."

"What else?" he prompted. "You're staring at your onion rings like they did you wrong."

"Cade," she said.

"Ah." He nudged his plate aside and reached for her hand. "I wondered if you'd picked up on that."

"You asked him to be part of the scene for a reason, didn't you? I mean, besides his bondage experience."

"I've done enough rope work to be able to manage the simple ties that he used on you last night," he confessed, toying with her fingers, his eyes her face. "It wouldn't have been as pretty, but I would've gotten the job done."

She nodded, having come to that conclusion herself. "So why have him help?"

"I wanted to see how you'd react to having another Top involved," he said, confirming her suspicions. "The stakes were low, since he wasn't technically playing with you—"

"He wasn't?"

Nick shook his head. "More acting as an assistant."

"It didn't feel like that to me," she muttered.

"Really?" He cocked his head. "How did it feel?"

She frowned, considering. "Okay, I guess he wasn't. It just felt like he was part of things, and…"

"And?"

"He kissed me." She looked up at him. "That's not assisting."

"No, it not," he allowed, a small smile on his lips. "You told me last night that you liked it. Is that still true?"

She fought the urge to squirm. "Yes."

"I thought so."

"It was partly the circumstances," she said carefully, trying to put her feelings into words. "I was already worked up, we were already in scene."

"All true. Are you sexually attracted to Cade?"

She blew out a breath. "You know I am."

"I still want you to say it."

"Fine." She huffed out a breath. "Yes, I am sexually attracted to Cade."

"Thank you for being honest."

"Are you doing this just to mess with me?" she demanded.

He laughed out loud. "No, but it's a nice side benefit. Look, I needed a hand last night, and you asked me to help you figure out if a threesome was something you actually wanted, or wanted to keep a fantasy. So, I asked Cade to help me with the rope to see how having him involved made you feel."

"So, the kiss was planned."

He shot her an amused look. "Baby girl, everything is planned."

"I should have known."

"But." He pursed his lips, considering her. "I think it was the wrong move."

She blinked. "Really?"

"You were in a punishment scene, and if you'd hated it or reacted badly, it would've impacted that. It turned out okay, but it was a bad idea to combine them."

"Oh."

He shifted, leaning forward over the table. "Also, if we're going to do this, it has to be with your fully informed, enthusiastic consent. It doesn't work otherwise. So, I think you need to figure this out for yourself."

"You do?"

He nodded. "If you want to talk it out, or have questions for me, I'm here. Otherwise, I'm going to let you work through it."

"Okay," she said, then paused. "Although..."

"Although?" he prompted.

"Sometimes I find it easier for you to force me into things I'm on the fence about," she confessed. "What if I want you to do that?"

He shook his head. "That's fine for some things, but not for this. Full and enthusiastic consent, remember?"

"I know, and you're right," she sighed. "Okay, I'll think about it."

"Good." He pushed back from the table and began to gather up the debris from their meal. "What do you want to do with the rest of the day?"

"Is it weird that I want a nap?" she asked, scooping up the takeout containers.

"You're still tired?"

"For some reason, I didn't sleep well last night," she informed him drily as she followed him into the kitchen.

"Gee, I wonder why?"

"Ha." She poked him in the back on the way to the recycling bin.

"Do you want company for your nap?"

She glanced back at him. "You hate taking naps in the middle of the day."

"But I like being with you," he told her, looping his arm around her from behind. "And if you nap on the sofa instead of the bed, I can put on that documentary on Galileo I've been meaning to watch."

"That will put me to sleep for sure," she said with a laugh. She turned in his arms and linked her fingers together behind his neck. "Throw in a foot rub and you've got yourself a deal."

"I was thinking you could lay your head in my lap," he suggested with that sexy smile that made her heart sigh and her pussy wet.

"If my head is in your lap, I won't get my nap and you won't get to watch your documentary," she informed him tartly, mentally admonishing her pussy to chill. *Jeez, give a girl some recovery time.*

"True. Okay. One foot rub, coming up." He gave her butt an affectionate pat. "You can put your head in my lap later."

"Work, work, work," she muttered, and jumped when he patted her ass harder.

"For that, you can finish cleaning up," he informed her, and landed one more slap on her ass before moving to the living room.

"Work, work, work," she called after him, laughing, and hurried to put the recycling away.

There was a foot rub waiting with her name on it.

* * * *

As March slid in to April and April to May, she did think about it. A lot. It still came up when they had sex—double penetration, the dirty talk about sharing her with someone else—but other than that he was true to his word and kept his silence.

It was driving her crazy.

"Maybe he's messing with you again," Sadie suggested. It was Wednesday, and Sadie was hosting Whine and Wine Wednesday at her apartment. They did it at least once a month, more if they could manage it, the venue changing depending on who felt like hosting. Sadie often volunteered, and though her apartment was small compared to Amanda's house or Rebecca's loft, no one complained.

It was the company that mattered, after all.

"I don't think so," Rebecca mused, nibbling on a cracker and nursing her glass of wine. Nick had implemented a rule that if she was driving, her alcohol intake was limited to one drink, and she'd learned to savor it. "I think he's really leaving it up to me."

"That doesn't mean messing with you isn't a nice side benefit," Amanda pointed out, a glass of Merlot in hand. "Doms are good multitaskers."

"That's the fucking truth," Rebecca muttered.

"So?" Sadie reached for the platter on her tiny coffee table, snagging a small wedge of cheese and a slice of prosciutto. "What are you going to do?"

"Well, I'm still thinking it over," Rebecca said, "but I'm pretty sure I'm going to ask my boyfriend to double team me with another Dom."

Olivia, a sweet submissive with honey-blonde hair and soft hazel eyes walked into the room, a fruit tray in her hand. "What'd I miss?"

"She wants to get double teamed," Amanda said, and shifted on the sofa to make room.

Sam, the lone man in their midst, followed Olivia out of the kitchen. Tall and slim, with salt-and-pepper hair and a quick, engaging grin, he set a plate of vegetables and dip on the already overcrowded coffee table. "I see we're getting to the good stuff fast tonight," he observed, and with nowhere else to sit, parked himself on the floor.

"I have a question." Sadie raised her hand. "Who's the third?"

"Oh, right." Rebecca cleared her throat. "Cade."

"Nice," Sadie said, and tapped her wineglass to Rebecca's. "He's smokin' hot, and there's a high 'yes, Sir' factor there."

"I have a little crush on him," Rebecca said, her cheeks heating at the confession.

"Don't we all," Olivia said with a sigh.

"I don't mean like I want to date him, or anything," Rebecca hastened to add as laughter rolled through the room. "But..."

"You'd be happy to ride him like you stole him," Sadie put in.

"Under these specific circumstances, yes." Rebecca sipped her wine to wet her throat. "I don't know him very well, but I like him, and Nick trusts him."

"I think Cade's a good choice," Olivia chimed in. "He's sweet."

"Super sweet," Sadie agreed. "He's helping her with Nick's birthday gift."

"What's Nick's birthday gift?" Amanda wanted to know.

"Photographs," Rebecca supplied, feeling a little silly. "Nick kept saying after that bondage scene we did at the St. Patrick's Day party that he wished he'd taken pictures before he dismantled me."

"Interesting turn of phrase," Sam murmured into his wine.

"Sadie knows a photographer, and I asked Cade to tie me up for it." She turned to Sadie. "Are you still good to help me with hair and makeup?"

"Yep. Cleared my day for it."

Amanda leaned forward. "Cade's going to tie you up so you can have fetish photos taken for Nick's birthday?"

Sam grinned. "It sounds even dirtier out loud. Two Doms, no waiting."

"Three holes, no waiting," Sadie snickered, and ducked when Rebecca threw a cracker at her.

"You're all a bunch of perverts." Rebecca popped a cracker in her mouth and tried not to wish for another glass of wine. "It's really not a big deal. Just a little fantasy fulfillment between friends."

"Uh-huh. What's your fantasy again?" Amanda wanted to know.

Rebecca selected a slice of cheese to nibble on. "Just your basic 'be a good little slut for Daddy and fuck his friend' scenario."

"With double penetration," Sadie pointed out.

"With double penetration," Rebecca echoed with a laugh.

"Well, then." Sam raised his wineglass in a toast, dimples popping in his cheeks when he smiled. "Here's to double penetration."

"To double penetration!" everyone chorused.

Chapter Ten

The third Friday in May was sunny and bright, and Rebecca rode the elevator to Nick's office with a sense of giddy anticipation. She wore an overcoat despite the warm weather, a thin black number that buttoned up to the neck and fell to mid-calf, successfully hiding the outfit she'd meticulously selected for today's surprise visit.

She got off the elevator, shifting the large packages she held. She noted with relief that the receptionist was on the phone, preventing a long chat, and simply sent her a wave and slid into the corridor leading to the offices.

She nodded and smiled at acquaintances as she passed, but kept moving. She'd worked for Saint Innovations for three years, so there were plenty of familiar faces, but she wasn't interested in catching up with former colleagues at the moment.

She'd timed her arrival to just before five o'clock, knowing all but the most die-hard employees would already be heading for the door on a sunny Friday afternoon. By the time she reached the end of the hall, the floor was all but deserted.

She approached the reception area outside Nick's office, and the desk that used to be hers, with a smile for its current occupant. "Is the coast clear?"

Kit lifted her head with a smile. "There you are. I thought Grace might have caught you."

"She would have, but she was on the phone," Rebecca said with a laugh.

"Lucky break." Kit nodded her elegant blonde head at the packages Rebecca held. "Want a hand with those?"

"I'm not sure what to do with them," Rebecca confessed. "I'd like to hide them in the office, but I can leave them behind the desk out here if he's in there."

"You're in luck." Kit rose from her desk walked to the door of the inner office, neat in a pair of black slacks and a blue blouse. "He's down at the lab, harassing Nate about something."

"Perfect." Rebecca hurried in after her. "Maybe the closet?"

"I'll get the door." Kit opened the door to the narrow closet where Nick kept an emergency change of clothes, and Rebecca quickly tucked both packages away. "I ordered up a couple of sandwiches, just in case you get hungry later. They're in the mini fridge with a six pack of beer."

"You're a better assistant than I ever was," Rebecca told her.

"Not being secretly in love with my boss helps," Kit replied with a laugh, her unusual eyes—one green, the other blue—dancing. "Do you want to hang up your coat?"

"I'll keep it on," Rebecca said, only blushing a little as she met her friend's knowing gaze. "It's, um, part of the surprise."

"And on that note," Kit drawled, "I'll get out of your way."

"I really appreciate this, Kit," Rebecca said, following her out to the desk.

"It's no trouble at all," Kit assured her, shouldering her purse. "Housekeeping usually comes by around nine o'clock, but I told them Nick's working on a sensitive project and to skip his office tonight. You should probably still lock the door, though."

"Seriously, I'm telling him to give you a raise."

"I wouldn't say no," Kit said with a wink. "Y'all have fun, now."

Rebecca waited until Kit's footsteps had faded down the hall, then reached for the belt on her coat. She peeled it off and hung it in the closet, then smoothed her hands down her clothes. She'd chosen the narrow black pencil skirt and fuzzy white sweater because while they were perfectly appropriate office attire, they were also sexy as fuck. The skirt hugged her hips and thighs, and the pushup bra—the one she would never, ever wear to work—shoved her tits almost out of the scoop neckline of the sweater.

She'd paired the pushup bra with matching panties and a garter belt. Seamed stockings and a pair of sky-high heels that she'd borrowed from Amanda—another thing she'd never wear to work, she liked her feet too much to put them through that for an entire day—completed the outfit, and the bright red soles of the Louboutins were an exact match for her lipstick.

She'd debated whether or not to put her hair back in a sleek tail, as was her habit for work, or leave it down for a sexier look. In the end she'd decided to pull it back, just to make the fantasy a bit more real—and to give Nick a handle.

With a little shiver of anticipation at the thought—honestly, she could've skipped the panties entirely for all the good they were doing her—she slipped into Kit's chair to wait.

And just in time, because heavy footsteps sounded down the hall, and a moment later, Nick came strolling in.

He'd shed his suit jacket during the day, and rolled up the sleeves of his crisp white shirt. He wasn't wearing a tie, and the top button on the shirt was undone, revealing the hollow of his throat. Charcoal-gray slacks rode on his hips, and the thin leather belt holding them up gave her ideas.

Delicious, depraved ideas.

He was so focused on the papers in his hand that he walked past her and into his office without a glance, closing the door behind him.

She stared at the wood, a bubble of laughter welling up in her throat. Of all the reactions she'd thought he'd have to her sitting at her old desk, she'd never imagined a scenario in which he wouldn't even notice her.

She was wondering what to do next when the intercom clicked on. "Kit, will you get me the file on the Dornbecker project, please?" he asked, and clicked off before she could reply.

The Dornbecker file was no doubt locked in the small file room behind the desk, the one that she no longer had a key to. But there was a small stack of Manila folders on the edge of the desk, empty and waiting to be filled. She grabbed one, stuffed some blank paper from the printer into it, and carried it into his office.

She took a moment to lock the door behind her and started across the floor. The shoes were half a size too big, forcing her to walk slowly and deliberately to his desk. He didn't look up, all his attention on the papers in front of him, so when she tossed the file smack in the middle of them, she had the pleasure of seeing him jump.

"What the hell?" His head shot up, a scowl already in place that turned to surprise, then pleasure as he registered who was standing in front of him. "Rebecca? What are you doing here?"

"Bringing you your file, Mr. Saint," she said smoothly, injecting just a hint of *fuck you* into her voice. "Though if you bark at me like that through the intercom again, you can get it yourself."

He hadn't barked at her through the intercom. His request had been respectful and courteous, even a 'please' at the end. But when she'd been his assistant, his requests had often had an edge to them. In fact, most of the time he'd been downright rude, grumpy and annoyed by unrequited lust.

She raised an eyebrow and favored him with the kind of smile she'd often employed while working for him—polite, vague, and entirely fake. "Will there be anything else, or can I go now?"

His eyes had lost the roundness of shock, and he was regarding her with the stone poker face that had allowed her to believe he had no feelings for her whatsoever for three years. But there was a gleam in his pale blue eyes that had never been there before, a predatory light that made him look like a wolf on the hunt.

And she was the prey.

"No, Ms. McBride, you cannot." He dropped his pen on his desk and leaned back, steepling his fingers together as he watched her with that inscrutable icy gaze. "Explain yourself."

"Excuse me?" she replied, fighting to keep her voice steady. It was hard, because she wanted to fall to her knees and beg for his cock. "What, exactly, am I supposed to explain?"

"Your attire," he replied, sharp gaze raking her from head to toe. She wasn't sure if he could see all the way to her feet with the massive desk in the way, but it sure felt like he could. "You really think this is appropriate for work?"

She looked down at the skirt and sweater as though she was giving the question serious consideration and not just hiding a giddy grin. He'd leapt right into the fantasy, and she was delighted to play her part.

Schooling her features into a defiant sneer, she lifted her head again. "It's a skirt and sweater, Mr. Saint."

"It's slutty, Ms. McBride."

"I beg your pardon?"

"Slutty," he repeated, enunciating the word sarcastically. "You look like you're about to shoot a secretarial-themed porno, for God's sake."

"Could you be any more insulting?" she asked, crossing her arms over her chest and shoving her tits up. They were already in danger of spilling out of the neckline of the sweater, now they were almost up to her chin. "This is a perfectly respectable outfit."

"Respectable, my ass," he shot back, and stood up so fast his chair fell over backward. He stalked around the desk like a lion tracking a gazelle. "Change your clothes, and while you're at it, change your attitude."

"My attitude?"

"Your attitude," he barked. "I've put up with your insubordination for months because you're good at your job, but that stops now. You either show me the respect due me as your boss, or there will be consequences."

"What, are you going to fire me?" she sneered, forcing herself to stand still as he prowled toward her. *Holy shit, this is hot.* "You can't run this place without me and you know it."

"No, I'm not going to fire you." He stopped in front of her. "I'm going to spank you."

"Spank me?" she sputtered, trying with all her might to stick to the script instead of flinging herself across the desk and begging for it. "Have you completely lost touch with reality?"

"I'm fed up," he snapped. "With your smart mouth and your short skirts—"

"This skirt is below my *knees*, asshole," she informed him tartly.

"—and your bitchy, disrespectful attitude," he finished. He lifted a finger in warning. "One more word, just one, and I'll put you over that desk and turn your ass red."

"Who the *hell* do you think you are?" she began hotly, then broke off with a shriek when he grabbed her arm. "What are you doing?"

"I warned you," he said grimly and yanked her forward. She had to scramble in the skinny heels, the narrow skirt hindering her even further. When they reached the front of his desk he bent and, with one swoop of his arm, cleared the papers off the surface. Before the last piece had fluttered to the floor, he had one broad hand in the middle of her back, forcing her down.

She was all but pressed to the blotter when she remembered she was supposed to be resisting. "Get your filthy hands off of me," she snarled, rearing up. The move took him by surprise, and she nearly twisted out of his grasp. But he recovered quickly, using both hands on her upper arms to shove her back down, and this time he grabbed her wrist, twisting it up behind her back and effectively pinning her there.

"You can't do this," she said, shoving aside the cloud of lust that had taken over her brain. *Stay in character, Becca.* "I'll sue your fucking ass off."

"Shut up," he said mildly, his grip on her wrist just shy of bruising. Something slipped over her hand to circle her wrist, some kind of fabric. She turned her head and saw the blue silk tie he'd put on that morning. He'd formed a basic slip knot and looped it around her wrist, and was now stretching her arm across the desk.

She knew exactly what he was doing. The drawer pulls on the massive desk were brass, and she'd thought more than once during her tenure as Nick's assistant that they would've made excellent hard points if they weren't attached to removable drawers. He looped the ends of the tie through the handle on the top left drawer, tying a fast knot that left plenty of play in the fabric, and she gave it an experimental wiggle. The slip knot wasn't a great choice for long-term bondage, but he'd drawn the tails of the tie up through her palm, making it easy for her to hold on to the fabric to manage the tension.

She fisted her hand around the silk, keeping it loose around her wrist as he stalked to the closet. Her heart clutched when he flung open the door, worried the packages at the bottom would catch his attention, but he didn't even seem to notice them. He pulled out one of his back up ties, gold this time, then walked back and grabbed her other arm. She waited until he'd looped it around her wrist and tied it around the handle on the top right drawer of his desk before she started to struggle.

"You won't get away with this," she warned him, yanking her arms hard enough to make the brass clank. She gripped the silk hard so it wouldn't tighten around her wrists and yanked again, and this time the whole desk seemed to rattle.

"I told you to shut up," he said, walking back to the open closet. "If you know what's good for you, you'll do it."

"Fuck you," she sputtered, even as her panties grew wetter. This was going even better than she'd imagined, and she'd imagined it going *great*. "You're out of your goddamn mind."

"I must be, otherwise I'd have done this years ago," he said, and turned back to her with another tie in his hands and a gleam in his eyes.

She jerked her head away when he came at her with the tie, but he simply followed, forcing the silk between her teeth. She grumbled and growled for form, and he forced her head back with a hard yank. "Since you can't follow simple fucking instructions," he explained, knotting the silk at the back of her head, below her ponytail, "we'll do it this way."

She was struggling in earnest now, yanking at her arms and tossing her head in an instinctive effort to dislodge the gag. It got her exactly nowhere, which just made it hotter.

Then he pulled a pair of scissors from his desk drawer, and she froze.

They were old-fashioned shears, all metal, with wickedly pointed blades and gleaming handles. He'd had those scissors for years, he'd told her once, preferring them over the ones they were making now, with plastic handles and lighter metal. They weighed a ton and made an ominous sound whenever he used them, and their sudden appearance brought the first real trickle of anxiety she'd had since she'd walked in the door.

"Now that you can't interrupt," he began, circling behind her, scissors in hand. "I'll continue. This skirt is inappropriate."

"Ib ibs mob," she mumbled through the gag.

"It is so," he replied, proving he was fluent in Gagged Submissive. "It clings to your ass, and it's so fucking tight you can barely walk. It makes you look vulgar and cheap."

"Heep?" she screeched.

"Cheap," he repeated. "You won't wear it again. Am I understood?"

"Huck ooo."

"Wrong answer," he replied calmly.

A loud, metallic snick of the scissors made her freeze, and the slight tug at the bottom of her skirt had her sucking in a shocked breath. Then there was a loud rip, a cold blast of air on her newly bared skin, and he yanked the ruined remnants of her favorite skirt from between her stomach and the edge of the desk and tossed it down in front of her.

She did not have to fake her scream of outrage.

"Now then," he said, ignoring her renewed struggles. "Let's talk about this sweater."

Oh, you better not, she thought, and fisted one hand, ready to thump it three times on the desk to safeword out if he even *hinted* at cutting this sweater. The skirt was replaceable—if he'd ripped it up the back seam, it might even be reparable—but she'd had this sweater for almost ten years and she knew, she *knew,* there was no way she'd be able to find another.

"The sweater," he went on, "isn't the problem, I don't think. You've worn it to work dozens of times, and your tits have never been falling out of it before today. So, what's different?"

He slid his hand under the sweater, warm and hard against her back, to toy with the band of her bra. "Did you wear a pushup bra to work today, Ms. McBride?"

She didn't bother to answer, just held her breath as he danced his fingertips along the edge of the strap.

"I think you did." He tsked, his disappointment clear. "It's going to have to go, too."

The strap across her back gave way, and the cups fell away from her breasts. It was almost a relief—that thing was *tight*—but she should've known it wouldn't end there.

"Since your hands are bound, and there's no way I'm cutting you loose just yet," he continued, "I'm afraid I'll have to use these."

He snapped the scissors close to her ear, and she instinctively flinched away. His hand delved into the wide neckline of the sweater to grab the elastic strap at her shoulder, and the cold metal of the shears slid against her skin. One quick snip, then he was repeating it on the other side before tugging the ruined bra away and tossing it on top of the ruined skirt.

She tried to drum up some outrage. That was the game, after all, and dammit, that bra had cost her a freaking fortune. But outrage was not what she was feeling.

He circled the desk to stand in front of her, tall and built and very into her little surprise role play, if the tent in his slacks was anything to go by. Her mouth watered behind the gag, and she wondered if he'd be fucking her face soon. She didn't think so. He'd have to literally sit on the desk to make that work in her current position. He could untie her, of course, but she'd fantasized so long about him tying her to this desk that she sincerely hoped he wouldn't.

"Nice tits," he drawled, and she looked down to see that they'd all but fallen out of the neckline of the sweater. Her nipples were still contained somehow, but he took care of that quickly enough, reaching in and scooping them out. Her boobs lay on the desk blotter, slightly smashed by the way she was leaning into the desk, swollen and heavy, her nipples diamond hard with arousal.

"Your tits are on my desk, Ms. McBride," he drawled mockingly.

You put them there, Mr. Saint, she thought, and tried to glare at him through the haze of lust.

Since his response was to laugh, she didn't figure she pulled it off. Then he unbuckled his belt, and she didn't care.

"Where was I?" he asked, drawing the thin, supple leather through his belt loops with a quick flick of his wrist and a slither of sound. "Oh, yes. Consequences."

He walked back around the desk, belt in hand, while she stared at the pile of ruined clothing in front of her. The way she was bent over meant she couldn't turn to follow his progress, so she tried to guess where he was by what she could hear.

"Pretty lingerie," he commented, and by the sound of his voice, he was standing directly behind her. "You always wear stockings and garters?"

She didn't answer, assuming the question was rhetorical. The hard slap of his hand on her panty-covered ass told her otherwise. "I asked you a question, Ms. McBride."

She nodded her head in a frantic yes, panting a little as the sting and the heat spread. He'd hit her hard enough to rock her forward into the desk, the kind of smack he usually only delivered after a thorough warm-up.

"Yes, you do," he confirmed, and smacked her other cheek just as hard as the first.

No, there would be no warm-ups today.

"That's for dressing like a slut to work," he informed her. "I don't care what you do on your own time, Ms. McBride, but you will conduct yourself with appropriate decorum in my office. Is that clear?"

She nodded, ponytail swaying. She was breathing hard now, the gag soaked through. Something else was soaked through, too, and she wondered how long it would take him to notice.

"Are you...*wet?*" he asked, outraged, and she stifled a laugh as she shook her head, clearly and boldly lying.

"Save your lies for someone who cares," he snapped, his voice closer now but also lower, as though he'd bent down to get a good look at the state of her panties. "I can see how wet you are. This excuse for underwear is fucking soaked."

The underwear in question—which had also cost a fortune—was a pair of sheer black bikini panties that technically covered her entire ass while in effect covering nothing at all. She'd intended to buy the thong that matched the bra, but Sadie had convinced her that a pair of demurely cut panties in sheer fabric was a much more powerful visual.

Thank you, Sadie.

"Goddammit, you're practically dripping on the carpet," he snapped, and he sounded so angry that a trickle of unease wormed its way into her belly.

"This is completely unacceptable," he continued. She flinched at the touch of cold steel on her hip. "I don't care that they're hidden by your clothes, you will not wear such garments to work."

There was a quick snip, then her panties fell away from her right hip, and a heartbeat later the steel slid against her left. One more snip, then he was pulling the thin swatch of delicate fabric away from her body and cool air rushed over her wet, heated pussy.

She couldn't see what she looked like, but she could imagine it. The shoes with their tall, skinny heels boosted her height so her ass was higher than the desk, bare now but for the garter belt framing it. The garters were little more than ribbons, with little bows just above where they snapped onto the tops of the stockings. Stockings that were, per her lover's preference, sheer with a thin, black seam running down the back of her thigh and calf before disappearing into the heel of her shoe.

The fact that she still wore her sweater only added a layer of debauchery.

"I'm very disappointed in you, Ms. McBride," he said, yanking her attention back to him. His voice was low and firm, every inch the stern Daddy she'd fallen in lust with when she had started working for him all those years ago. Every inch the stern Daddy she loved so deeply now.

"I take no pleasure in what I'm about to do," he continued, the sheer lust in his voice making a mockery of the words, and she barely held back a snort of disbelief. "I hope you understand that my goal is to make you understand what's expected of you here, and help you make better choices in the future."

She jerked at her bonds, mostly for form, but also because the pent-up need inside her was driving her to move, to seek out the pressure and the friction that would bring relief. She leaned into the desk, crushing her breasts beneath her, and wiggled her ass in the air.

His choked laugh made her grin around the gag.

"You brought this on yourself," he warned.

The whistle of leather slicing through the air reached her ears a split second before the belt hit her ass. The impact shoved her into the desk and fire blazed across her skin, the bright, sharp sting of it driving the breath from her lungs. The shock had barely faded before he did it again, the pain of the second overlapping the first. He paused for a second, perhaps giving her time to protest, but when she merely tightened her fists on his ties and boosted her ass higher, he went to work.

Over and over the belt fell, the kiss of the leather on her tender skin both a benediction and a penance. The blows came so quickly they blended into one another, pain layered upon pleasure, pleasure upon pain. By the time he dropped the belt and pressed into her, the soft, silky fabric of his slacks like sandpaper against her tenderized ass, she was shaking with need. She couldn't be sure, but the possibility that she actually *was* dripping onto the carpet was high.

He grabbed her ponytail and pulled, forcing her head back as he draped himself over her back. "Have you learned your lesson, Ms. McBride?"

She struggled a little in his hold, against her bonds, mumbling incoherently through the gag. His dick was hard against her ass, hot even through the fabric of his pants, and she wanted it inside her badly enough to beg for it.

"No, I can see you haven't," he said, his breath hot on her neck. "Even tied up and helpless, you're still fighting for the upper hand."

She had absolutely no interest in the upper hand, and he knew it. But that was the game, so she bucked her hips back into him as though she was trying to throw him off.

He gave a harsh laugh and leaned into her so hard her knees almost buckled. "No, you haven't learned a fucking thing," he snarled, and gave her hair a yank before letting go so abruptly she nearly banged her face on the desk. "I should've have known there was only one way to get through to you."

There was the quick, metallic slide of a zipper, the rustle of fabric, then his hands were on her ass. His fingers dug in hard as he spread her cheeks apart, making her hiss in pain, then the broad, blunt head of his cock was right where she needed it.

He pushed forward, breaching her slick and swollen labia, stopping when he was barely inside her. She held her breath, waiting for more, but he didn't move. The muscles there flexed, as though they could draw him in, and he laughed.

"Eager little slut," he said, digging his fingers in harder. "You want my cock?"

She nodded frantically, giving up the game without qualm. "Please," she mumbled around the gag. "Please, Daddy."

"What was that, slut?" he asked mockingly, pulling back so he was barely touching her. She whined and tried to follow, but the ties on her wrists and his hands on her hips held her ruthlessly in place. "Say it again, I couldn't hear you."

"Please," she repeated, fighting to enunciate around the cloth in her mouth. She inched her feet farther apart, spreading her thighs in a silent plea. "Please."

"Fuck, look at that cunt." He shifted his hands on her ass, using his thumbs to pull her labia apart. She felt the cool wash of air and the hot wash of shame, and the coil of need inside her wound tighter.

"Get that ass back up," he demanded, and she arched her back to bring her hips higher. "There you go, that's what I want. Hold it just like that."

She locked her knees, her legs shaking with the effort to hold still, controlling the urge to buck back into him when he brought his cock back to her pussy. She expected him to tease her, to play with her a little bit before sliding his cock into her cunt, but he must have been just as impatient as she was, because he buried himself inside her with a hard, heavy thrust that actually lifted her out of her shoes.

She squealed into the gag, grunting a little as her hip bones hit the edge of the desk. Without the shoes, her toes barely brushed the floor, but it didn't seem to matter. Nick merely stepped forward, crowding her against the desk, and began to pound into her.

It was a loud, messy fuck, the sounds of it echoing around the room—the slap of skin on skin, guttural grunts and breathless squeals. There was the slick, wet slide of his cock pistoning in and out of her cunt, the thud every time he drove her into the desk. The brass handles on the drawers rattled, and the stapler bounced across the surface before crashing to the floor.

And through it all, he talked.

"You've got a greedy fucking cunt, baby girl," he panted in her ear, pumping into her so fast and hard she could barely catch her breath. "You like how I fuck you?"

She nodded her head, grunting around the gag. His balls were slapping into her clit on every thrust, sending little sparks of sensation blasting through her. Her core felt heavy and tight, pressure and tension a hard fist in her belly.

"Yeah, you do. You like how I fuck you. That's it, give Daddy that pussy. It's mine, isn't it? My slutty pussy."

He sped up, racing now. Sweat slickened their thighs, dripped off his forehead to splash against the back of her neck. "Going to come in that slutty fucking pussy, little girl, and you're going to come with me."

That wasn't going to be a problem. She was already close, teetering on the edge. But the slap of his balls on her clit wasn't enough—she needed something more.

"Yeah, you're going to come, and I'm going to fill you up. You'll be leaking my come for days. Come on, slut," he urged. "Come on and come."

The words accomplished what nothing else did, the dirty, filthy punch of them shoving her over that edge, and with a scream that made her thankful he'd gagged her, she came.

"Oh, fuck yeah," he ground out, hips flying as he reached for his own orgasm. "Squeeze that pussy on me, baby girl. Shit, I fucking love your fucking pussy, gonna fill it up."

He let out a shout and came, flooding her with the wet heat of his orgasm. He kept fucking her, the squelch of his cock lewd and vulgar and so fucking hot she came again, her pussy pulsing hard around him.

When it was over, she laid her head on the desk between her outstretched arms and wondered how the hell they'd gotten through three years of working together without doing that.

Chapter Eleven

"Thanks for my birthday present," Nick murmured an hour later.

Rebecca picked up her head to peer at him through heavy eyes. "That wasn't your birthday present."

He shifted slightly to see her better. They were lying on the couch in his office, the remains of their dinner on the floor behind them. She wore his spare shirt over her only remaining undergarments—the garter belt and stockings—and a sleepy smile. "It wasn't?"

She shook her head. Her hair, free from its ponytail, slithered over his bare chest. "No. Well, not your only birthday present, anyway."

"I get more?" he asked, delighted.

"Lots more."

"Excellent. I've always wanted to lay you out on my desk and eat your pussy until you scream." He slid his hand under the hem of the borrowed shirt to cup her bare ass. She winced a little at the contact, and he quirked his lips into a grin. "Does your butt hurt, love?"

The look she gave him was sardonic. "Someone went to town on it with a belt, so yes, it's a bit tender."

"Aw." He squeezed one firm cheek just to hear her squeak. "Poor baby."

She squealed and jerked in his hold, trying in vain to dislodge his hand. "Red, red, red!"

He let go, laughing as she pouted at him through the curtain of her hair.

"You're so mean, Daddy."

"Yes," he agreed soberly.

She snickered, wiggling around so she lay on top of him. "You'll be sorry you were so mean to me when you see what I got you," she told him with a haughty sniff, and slid out of his arms and off the couch.

He let her go, his curiosity roused when she walked to the closet. "You brought them here? I thought we were doing presents at dinner tomorrow."

She glanced over her shoulder. "Your parents and your brother will be there."

"So?"

"So, these presents are not family friendly," she told him, and emerged with two packages, one large and flat like a painting, and the other thicker, like a book. "I got you something else, something you can open in front of your parents, but these are for your eyes only."

"Well, now I'm intrigued." He rose to take the big one from her, eyeing them both curiously. They were wrapped in plain brown paper and tied with twine. "Fancy wrapping paper."

"I will remind you that I carried these through your office, where many people know your birthday is tomorrow. If they were wrapped in 'happy birthday' paper, you'd be fielding a lot of questions on Monday."

He sat back down, the large package in hand. "Good point."

"Thank you." She snagged the scissors off the desk and rejoined him on the couch. "Open the big one first."

He glanced at her as he took the scissors from her, trying to gauge her mood. She was excited, practically vibrating with anticipation, but there were nerves, too. She was chewing on her bottom lip, and she'd curled up with her feet under her, unconsciously making herself small.

Curious about what she could've gotten him that would make her so anxious, he quickly snipped through the twine. The paper fell away, revealing a large, framed photograph. He recognized the brick walls of the loft in the background, and the subject in the center of the photo was— "Rebecca."

"Do you like it?" she asked, her voice tentative. "You said several times after St. Patrick's Day that you wished you'd taken pictures, so I just thought..."

Her voice trailed away, and some part of him realized that she was waiting for his reaction, but he couldn't stop staring at the photo.

Rebecca stood in the center of the shot, one foot poised in front of the other, as though she were taking a step toward the camera. She had on the same fancy shoes she'd worn for the St. Patrick's Day party at James and Amanda's, the satin bow drooping artfully across her instep. Her legs were bare, the cleft between them shadowed by the way she was posed, though the wild thatch of pubic hair at the top of her mound was clearly visible. Her arms were raised, her hands in her tumbled mass of dark hair. The pose lifted her breasts slightly, a thin swatch of skin between them and the top of the ropes that circled her torso from her ribcage to the top of her hips in a bondage corset just like the one Cade had wrapped around her on St. Patrick's Day.

She was staring right at the camera, her lips curved and her eyes sly, a woman well aware of her power and more than capable of wielding it.

It was breathtaking.

"You don't like it," she said, and the dismay in her voice finally jolted him out of his trance.

"I love it." He turned to her, his stomach dropping at the look on her face. "It's the most beautiful thing I've ever seen."

Her eyes lit. "Really?"

"Really." He turned back to stare at it. "How did you do this? When did you do this?"

"Last month, when Nate dragged you to Kansas City to look at that lab he wants to buy."

"Waste of time," he muttered absently. "Who took the picture?"

"Sadie has a friend, Penny. She just started her own business, so she gave me a bit of a break on the fee in exchange for using some of the shots in her portfolio."

He nodded absently, then the words hit. "There are other pictures?"

"Lots more." She tapped a finger on the black frame. "Turn this over."

He flipped it around. "A double-sided frame?"

"That's the last shot we got," she explained while he stared. "Penny and Cade had something else they wanted to do, but we'd been at it for a few hours, and it turns out that posing for pictures is exhausting. I was kind of done, so they came up with this."

"Cade was there?"

She nodded. "He did the rigging. We used the rope you bought from him after St. Patrick's Day."

"I see that." This shot was in color, and the bright green of the rope seemed to pop out of the picture. She was lying on her side in the middle of their bed, the white sheets rumpled and tangled under her, with the rope piled over and around her.

Her hair was tangled on the pillow, her features soft. Her eyes looked sleepy, her makeup faded and smudged, and her mouth was bare. Her hand lay palm up on the pillow next to her, the fingers gently curled. Her other arm lay across her ribs, leaving her breasts bare but for the rope draped over them. Her nipples were no longer peaked but puffy and soft, like they often were after a night of loving.

He could just make out the faint marks circling her wrists and ankles, and the heavier ones on her thighs and waist. The first image showed a woman at the peak of her power, and this one showed the quiet aftermath.

He turned to look at her. "There's only one problem with this."

"What's that?"

"I want to hang them both."

She laughed. "We can get another frame. And if you want to get any of the other shots printed—"

"There are more?"

She handed him the second package, and he snipped through the string to find a leather portfolio filled with proofs. He paged through them, awed at the sheer volume of them. "She took a lot of shots. No wonder you were tired."

"Trust me, I have a newfound respect for fetish models. You really like them?"

"I love them." He set the portfolio aside to scoop her into his lap and yank her down for a kiss. "I love you. Thank you."

She leaned against him, her cheeks flushed with delight. "You're welcome."

He slid his hands under the shirt to cup her ass. "I can't believe you pulled this off without me knowing."

"I had help," she reminded him. "Sadie's a born sneak, and Cade was great."

"Remind me to thank them." He nuzzled her neck. "Although, I think Cade should be thanking me."

"Why?"

"Because he got to tie you up again," he murmured, nibbling his way to the open collar of the shirt.

"He was a perfect gentleman," she informed him in a prim little voice, and tilted her head back to give him better access.

"I'm sure he was." He undid the button between her breasts to nuzzle his way between them. "Did you have fun?"

"It was neat. Exhausting, but fun."

"I don't mean the photo shoot," he said against the hollow of her throat. "I meant with Cade."

"He was a perfect gentleman," she said again.

"And you have a crush on him." He nipped at her neck before she could speak, hard enough to make her jump. "Tell the truth and shame the devil."

"I never understood that saying. I mean, can the devil really feel shame?"

"Rebecca," he said warningly.

"What?" she asked innocently, then squeaked when he bit her again. "Oh, don't give me a hickey. I don't want to have to wear a turtleneck to work on Monday."

"Then stop stalling," he advised, and licked at the marks he'd just made.

"I might have a tiny, small, completely superficial and totally inconsequential crush on him."

"You could've just said yes," he informed her, amused when she huffed out an annoyed breath, and went to work on the buttons on her shirt.

"I could have, but in light of my next question, I wanted to be clear."

He had the shirt open now, the crisp white cotton framing her breasts. Her nipples were puffy and pale, like they'd been in the photo, and he wondered how long he could tease them before they puckered up. "What question is that?"

"Is he still your first choice for a third party?"

"A third party for what?" he asked absently, his attention on her left nipple. It was already starting to pucker, and he couldn't decide if he was disappointed or delighted.

"A third party for us," she said.

He pulled back to look at her face, her nipple momentarily forgotten. "You mean for a threesome?"

"Duh," she muttered.

"Smart ass," he said, and slapped the ass in question.

She reached back to rub her butt. "Ow."

He ignored her scowling pout. "You have something to tell me?"

Her cheeks flushed a delicate pink. "I know I've been thinking about it for a while."

"You're allowed to take your time," he told her. "There's no deadline."

"I know. And I appreciate you not pushing me. But I've been thinking about it a lot, and, well…I think I want to do it."

He quirked a brow at her choice of words. "You think, or you know?"

"I *know* I want to do it. But…"

"But?"

She sighed. "I'm worried."

"About boundaries," he said, smiling when she blinked at him in surprise. "I know you, love. You don't do well with 'take it as it comes' scenarios."

"I know." She frowned. "I really wish I could be a fly by the seat of my pants kind of gal, but I'm not."

His lips twitched. "Gal?"

"It's a word," she said with a defensive sniff. "Is it weird that I want to plan this out?"

"Not at all. Plans are good, as long as we build in some flexibility to allow for changes in circumstances, needs, etcetera."

"I can be flexible," she mused.

He gave her hip a pat. "Of course you can."

She narrowed her eyes. "I hear that sarcasm."

He laughed. "No sarcasm, I promise. You can be very flexible, but you have to feel safe first."

"Oh. I guess that's true."

"So, the question is, do you trust me to make you feel safe for this?"

"You always make me feel safe," she said, eyeing him carefully.

"Then I'll make plans."

A hint of trepidation edged into her smoky gray eyes, delighting him. "Do I get any say in this?"

"You get *all* the say in this," he assured her seriously. "We'll talk out what you want, what you don't want, what you need to feel safe and loved and protected."

"Oh. Good."

"Then Cade and I will figure out how to do all of that while fucking you into oblivion."

"Oh, good," she said again.

He laughed, gathering her close. "You trust me?"

She snuggled against him, her face buried in his throat. "I trust you."

"You love me?"

"I love you."

"I love you, too. Now be a good girl and go crawl under the desk."

"Under the desk?" She pulled back to look at him. "What happened to laying me out on top of it and eating my pussy until I scream?"

"We'll get to that. I have more than one Rebecca at Work fantasy," he explained.

"Really?" She grinned and slipped off his lap. "Me too."

"That's my girl," he said, and waited until she'd disappeared under the desk to follow.

* * * *

A week and a half later, Nick was up to his elbows in accounting reports when his intercom buzzed. "Mr. Saint, Mr. Hollis is here."

Nick glanced at the clock and groaned. "Shit, I didn't realize it was that late. Thanks, Kit. You can send him back."

"On his way," his assistant replied. "As is lunch."

"You're a gem," Nick told her.

"I know," she said smugly, and he was laughing when Cade walked through the door.

"What's so funny?"

"Just my assistant busting my balls," Nick said, rising to greet his friend.

"Yeah?" Cade returned the hug with a grin. "I like ball busters. Is she single?"

"As far as I know, but if you hit on her and she quits, I'll gut you with a spoon."

"Testy."

"Then Rebecca will kill you, because she'll have to find me someone new. Again."

"Dude, get an HR department," Cade said, then turned when door opened.

Kit stepped inside, neat as a pin in a pair of trim slacks and a thin sweater, pushing a small cart in front of her. It held takeout containers from Nick's favorite burger place, a selection of sodas, two glasses of sparkling crystal, and a small bucket of ice.

"Gentlemen," she said with a perfunctory nod for Cade, making her sleek blonde ponytail sway. "Lunch."

"Thanks, Kit." Nick moved to take the cart, only to have Cade smoothly nudge him out of the way.

"This looks great." He angled his head so his dark hair, longer now and tousled—probably because he'd forgotten to comb it, but still, it looked great—fell charmingly across his brow. He smiled at her. "Kit, is it?"

"To my friends," she said smoothly, a hint of amusement in her voice as Cade took the cart. She took a discreet step back, shifting her attention to Nick, her hands folded neatly in front of her. "Will there be anything else, Mr. Saint?"

Nick had to grin at the gentle but firm rejection of Cade's attempt at flirtation. "I think we're set. You can go ahead to lunch yourself. I'll see you at two for the meeting with accounting."

She inclined her head slightly. "Enjoy your lunch."

Cade let out a soft whistle as the door clicked smartly shut behind her. "Subtle, but hot. Does she always call you Mr. Saint?"

Nick was busy unpacking his burger, the scent making his mouth water. "She thinks it's unprofessional to call me by my first name if there are other people around."

Cade grabbed his own burger and took a seat at the small conference table by the window. "If I ask for her number on the way out, are you going to get pissy with me?"

"I don't think she's kinky, Cade."

Cade snagged a soda from the cart with a snort. "Like she'd tell you if she was."

Nick took his seat. "Good point. But if you cost me my assistant, I won't let you fuck my girlfriend."

Cade, who had taken huge bite of juicy hamburger, promptly choked. He grabbed a napkin and coughed into it, eyes watering, while Nick scooped ice into a glass and poured out a Coke.

"I didn't know that was an option," Cade wheezed, and took a throat-clearing guzzle of his own Coke, straight from the can.

"St. Patrick's Day didn't clue you in?"

Cade set his Coke down. His eyes were still watering a little. "You asked for my help with some bondage. Nothing unusual in that."

"I could've done those ties, and you know it," Nick scoffed. "Oh, and speaking of ties, thanks for helping Rebecca with my birthday present."

"My pleasure," Cade replied, and waggled his brows. "Sincerely."

Nick snorted out a laugh. "She said you were a perfect gentleman."

"Of course, I was. Doesn't mean I didn't enjoy myself. How'd the pictures turn out?"

"Amazing." Nick rose from his chair to go to his desk and snag the small frame that graced the corner.

Cade's eyebrows shot up. "You put one in your office? Bold, man."

"One of the safe-for-work ones." Nick handed it to him and resumed his seat.

"Oh, yeah." Cade studied the photo. "I remember this one. The photographer wanted to see what kind of angle she could get standing on one of the dining room chairs, and Sadie said something to make Becca laugh."

He stared at it a moment longer, then set it on the wide windowsill next to the table. "She looks good in red."

"Yeah, she does," Nick agreed, his eyes on Rebecca's image in the silver frame. She was bundled up in the red cashmere robe, curled in a corner of the sofa, her laughing face turned up to the camera.

"So." Cade bit into a French fry. "A threesome, huh?"

Nick pulled his attention away from the photo. "Yeah."

"I know you've done threesomes before, but has she?"

Nick shook his head. "Not yet. That's where you come in."

"Ah." He chewed thoughtfully. "I have to say, I didn't see this coming when you asked me to lunch today."

Nick glanced at his friend, noted the way his brows had drawn together. "If you're not up for it, it's fine. No pressure."

"No, I'm up for it," Cade assured him, but a frown furrowed his brow. "I assume the two of you have talked this out. Like, when you're dressed, not just when you're balls-deep and dirty talkin' your way to the finish."

Nick snorted. "Yes, jackass, we have."

"Just doing my due diligence," Cade said with an easy grin. "This is her idea or yours?"

"Hers. Well, it's her fantasy," he amended. "I offered to make it come true."

"Whose idea was it to ask me to be your special guest star?"

"That was a mutual decision, though you were definitely my first choice."

Cade picked up his burger again. "Why is that?"

"Three reasons. First, you and I have co-topped together before. With, if I do say so myself, great success."

"Very true."

"Second, I trust you. We thought about hiring a pro, and if this was just about sex we'd probably go that route. But for sex *and* a scene, I'm not putting Rebecca in a stranger's hands."

"Wise. And three?"

Nick gestured with a French fry. "She has a little crush on you."

"Does she, now?" Cade sat back, a slow smirk curving his mouth. "Well, well."

Nick just laughed. "This is a one-time invitation with an expiration date, so don't get your hopes up."

"My hopes are always up," Cade quipped, still smirking, and leaned forward to grab his soda. "But I'll keep my expectations reasonable. Do you want to do this at a club party?"

"No, something more private would be better. We could do it at our place, but I was thinking about getting hotel suite for it. You know, make it special. Plus..."

"Neutral territory?" Cade guessed, and Nick nodded. "Smart. What about when?"

"That pretty much depends on you, since you're the one most likely to have a scheduling conflict, but I think a Friday night would be best."

"You want the next day free for extended aftercare." Cade nodded thoughtfully. "I'll check my work schedule. What about the scene itself?"

"Nothing too complicated, at least regarding equipment. Basic bondage gear, and maybe a few other toys."

"If we're in a hotel, make sure one of them is a gag."

"Already on the list." Nick leaned back in his chair. "As for the setup, I have some ideas. Rebecca likes to be a good girl."

"I like good girls."

"She also likes to be a filthy little fucktoy."

Cade's grin was wolfish. "I like fucktoys, too."

"I know you do," Nick drawled, and checked his watch. "Do you have to rush off after lunch, or can you get into it now?"

"I've got some time." Cade polished off his burger. "Can I assume it'll be you and me working out the details, with the lovely Becca kept in the dark?"

"Not exactly in the dark." Nick rose to grab a legal pad and a pen from his desk. "She doesn't love surprises, so I need to give her enough to make her feel safe."

"But not so much that she's completely relaxed?" Cade guessed.

"Exactly." Nick put pen to paper. "First thing? Don't call Rebecca by her name."

Cade paused in the act of wiping his hands on a napkin, blinking in surprise. "You want me to call her 'slut' all night?"

"That'd probably work for her, actually," Nick said, amused. "But no, I just meant don't call her Rebecca. You usually call her Becca, and that's fine, but I'm the only one that uses her full name most of the time, and she likes that."

"Aw," Cade said with a grin. "Y'all are so cute."

Nick merely flipped him a middle finger and continued scribbling on the legal pad. "Your time will come, pal."

"I doubt it," Cade replied, and something in his tone had Nick frowning.

"You don't think there's someone out there for you?"

"Oh, they're out there." Cade's smile was firmly in place, but his eyes were shadowed. "But they're not for me."

Nick hesitated. He knew Cade was carrying a torch for someone who didn't return his affections, and though a dozen platitudes leapt to his tongue, he swallowed them all. Cade wouldn't talk about it, and anything he could say at this point would only sound hollow and, well, like a platitude. He wished though, not for the first time, that Cade's mystery love would come to their senses and make the man happy. He deserved it.

Before he could decide what to say, Cade shook his head. "Enough of that," he said with a wicked grin. "Tell me what I get to do to the lovely Becca."

And if, as they went over limits and set the parameters for the scene, the shadows never quite left Cade's eyes, Nick kept it to himself.

Chapter Twelve

On a Friday evening two weeks later, Nick sat in the parlor of a hotel suite in a small boutique hotel on the edge of downtown, frowning at his watch. "She's late."

Cade, seated across from him in chair with wood arms and needlepoint cushions that looked as though it had been designed for a doll house, looked up from his phone. "It's only six-fifteen," he pointed out reasonably.

"I told her to be here by six," Nick grumbled from the sofa, which matched the chair. He was pretty sure he looked ridiculous siting in it.

"Relax," Cade drawled, and returned to his phone, his thumbs tapping away at the screen. "She probably got hung up at work."

"We should've done this tomorrow," Nick muttered, and got up to pace.

"You're just mad she's working for someone else, and not you," Cade teased.

"If she were still working for me..."

"You probably wouldn't be together," Cade pointed out, still reasonable. "And you'd be home jerking off right now instead of getting ready to tag team your girlfriend."

"I hate it when you're reasonable," Nick complained, and Cade laughed.

"Relax, Daddy." Cade set his phone on the table beside his chair and leaned back, his brown eyes dancing. "It'll be fine."

"I just want this to be good for her," Nick explained, still pacing. "She's waited a long time for this fantasy."

"And you're making it come true," Cade replied. "But if you're that worried about it, I can go home. Then y'all can have nice vanilla sex in the missionary position with the lights out."

"Fuck you," Nick said, but he was laughing. When his phone dinged in his pocket, he dug it out, his breath easing out when he saw the message on the screen. "She's here. She's just parking the car."

"See?" Cade rose to his feet and stretched, then walked over to the wide window overlooking the street. "Do you need to go over the plan again, Mr. Preparedness?"

Nick sent Rebecca a quick text to remind her of the room number, then set his phone aside. "I'm good. How about you?"

"It's your rodeo, pal," Cade said in an easy tone that belied the gleam of anticipation in his eyes. "I'm just the guest wrangler."

"Cowboy metaphors? Really?"

"You're the one who put 'reverse cowgirl' on the play list," Cade reminded him.

"You can thank me later," Nick quipped, and they were grinning at each other when Cade's phone let out a soft chime.

"Guess I better turn this off," he said absently, and stepped over to pick it up.

Nick glanced at his watch, wondering how long it would take Rebecca to get to the suite, then crossed to the larger of the suite's two bedrooms and stepped inside for a last-minute glance around. His toy bag sat on the foot of the four-poster bed, within easy reach. A bottle of lube and a handful of condoms had been placed on the bedside table. Though he and Rebecca only used them for anal sex, they'd all agreed that everyone would suit up for tonight's party. The curtains had been drawn for privacy, and the bedside lamps turned on low.

Satisfied the room was ready, he turned back to Cade. "I think we're all set," he began, then frowned. Cade was staring at his phone, and he didn't look happy. "Something wrong?"

"No. I don't think." Cade glanced up, then back down. "Olivia's at my house."

Nick knew that Cade and Olivia were in a gaming group together that usually met at Cade's. "Are they having game night at your house without you?"

Cade shook his head. "She says she left Kyle."

"About fucking time," Nick muttered under his breath. He liked Kyle fine, and considered him a friend, but he'd never thought he and Olivia were right for each other. "Is she all right?"

Cade's thumbs were flying over the screen. "She says she's fine, just needs a place to crash for a couple of days."

Nick pursed his lips. "Rebecca and I have a guest room. Olivia's welcome to it."

"She can stay at my place as long as she needs to," Cade said, glancing up. "But I'll let her know she has options."

"Do you need to go?"

"What? No." Cade tapped at his phone for another moment, then set it down. "It's fine. She knows her way around my place. I'll see her when I get back."

Nick studied his friend's face for a moment, then nodded. "If you're sure."

"I'm sure," Cade said just as a knock sounded on the door. He grinned and resumed his seat in the ridiculously dainty chair. "Looks like it's showtime."

Nick walked to the door and laid a hand on the knob, then glanced back at Cade. "Ready?"

Cade leaned back in the chair in a casual pose. If it wasn't for the decidedly predatory gleam in his eye, he might have looked as though he were waiting for a bus. "Oh, yeah."

Nick spared a wolfish grin for his friend, then schooled his face into stern lines, and opened the door.

Rebecca stood outside the door to the suite, feeling frazzled, harried, disheveled, and decidedly unsexy.

Her 'low-key Friday' at work had turned into a nightmare of misplaced documents and scheduling screwups that had thrown the entire office into a tizzy. Her assistant had been too busy crying about how she couldn't afford to lose her job to actually do her job, the mailroom had a record of the package holding the missing documents being received but not delivered, and her boss, who had been the one to insist on original documents rather than electronic in the first place, had turned such a bright shade of purple she'd worried she might have to call the paramedics.

And to top it off, she'd had to personally go down to the mail room to find the missing envelope. She glanced down at her skirt and blouse, now dusty and wrinkled from the ten minutes she'd spent literally crawling around on the floor. She'd finally found the missing envelope not on the floor or behind a sorting bin, but under the mail room supervisor's leaky travel mug. The well-deserved tongue lashing she'd levied at the incompetent man had barely taken the edge off her temper, and her stockings had been so badly shredded, she'd had to throw them out.

Not exactly the mood she'd wanted to be in for her first threesome. But if anything could turn the disaster of a day around, surely it was hot sex with two skilled Doms.

She gave her skirt a tug in an attempt to smooth out the worst of the wrinkles, sighed when it did absolutely fuck all to help, and raised her hand to knock on the door.

When it swung open, Nick stood there looking at her with a grumpy look on his face. "You're late."

"I know," she sighed, and stepped forward to rest her head on his chest. Just because she could. "I'm sorry."

"You will be." His voice was a comforting rumble under her ear, even if the tone was menacing enough to have nerves jumping in her belly. He stroked his hands down her arms, over her back, brushing away the tension of the day. "Rough day at work?"

"I don't want to talk about it," she said, and nuzzled into his neck. He smelled so good, she just wanted breathe him in for a few hours. "I just want to forget it."

He chuckled and curled his hands around her upper arms. "Oh, we can help you with that," he drawled. "Can't we, Cade?"

"I think it could be arranged," a new voice chimed in, and Rebecca lifted her head to see Cade lounging in casual slacks and a simple black button down. His dark hair was long enough now to curl over his collar, and the look in his dark eyes was delightfully, deliciously predatory. Her heart rate kicked up a notch as awareness prickled her scalp, then she noticed the chair he was sitting on. A delicate, dainty thing, all spindly legs and needlepoint cushions. His muscular frame dwarfed it, and it looked as though it could collapse under him any minute.

She giggled at the image, and his eyes, normally so full of humor and warmth, narrowed fractionally. "Sorry, sorry," she managed, waving a hand in front of her face as though she could make the last few moments disappear. "It's just... that chair is ridiculous."

His grin flashed, though the edge remained. "I've been sitting in it for a while, waiting for you. It'll probably hold a while longer."

She didn't miss the slight emphasis on *waiting for you,* and tried to put a respectfully apologetic look on her face. "I'm sorry you had to wait."

"Hmm. A nice apology, but I don't know if it's enough." His gaze held hers for one heartbeat, two, then flicked over her head. "What do you think, Nick?"

"Oh, not nearly enough." Warm, hard fingers grasped her chin, lifting her face so she met Nick's bright blue eyes, and the expectant look in them. "You kept two Doms waiting, baby girl."

The rest of her miserable day slid away, replaced by anticipation. She sank to her knees, head up so her eyes stayed fixed on Nick's. Unless he said otherwise, he liked to see her eyes when they were in scene. "I'm sorry, Daddy," she said, her voice as strong as she could make it when she wanted nothing more than to melt into a puddle at his feet.

"Very nice," he rumbled, stroking a hand over her hair in approval. "Now, apologize to our guest."

She turned her head to look at Cade. He hadn't moved, but the look on his face was so intense that she hesitated. Nick's fingers tightened briefly on her head, in either comfort or correction—probably both—then fell away.

"Go on," he said, a thread of steel in his tone making it an unmistakable order.

She started to push to her feet, then changed her mind. Guided by instinct and the desire to show them how eager she was, she slowly fell forward so she rested on her hands and knees, and began to crawl.

Nick hissed out a breath behind her, and she paused to glance back over her shoulder. His eyes held surprise, yes, but also heat and a fierce kind of pride that made her wonder if she should crawl more often.

Bolstered by his obvious approval, she turned and continued across the room on her hands and knees.

The carpet under her was slightly rough, scraping at her bare legs. Cade remained still in the chair, his only movement the flicker of his eyes as he tracked her progress across the room. She stopped at his feet and sat back on her haunches, letting her hands rest on her knees. She looked up at him. "I'm sorry you had to wait for me, Sir."

The *Sir* just slipped out, but he liked it. She saw it in the way his eyes flared, the way his lips parted briefly before he tightened them into a hard line again, staying in character. The Cade she knew was friendly, quick with banter or a joke. He was genial and courteous, kind and considerate. But that wasn't the Cade sitting in front of her now.

This Cade had edges, sharp ones that were so boldly obvious, she wondered how she'd ever missed them.

"I believe you," he rumbled, pulling her attention back to his face. His jaw was tight under the scruff of his beard, his cheekbones somehow sharper, like his face had changed shape to match the sinister intent. "But I did have to wait, didn't I?"

She swallowed hard, her eyes automatically dropping to the floor at his tone. She recognized Disappointed, Disapproving Dom when she heard it, and she knew the appropriate response was *not* to giggle. So she kept her face down and spoke in a soft, quiet voice that she hoped sounded meek and subservient rather than gleefully anticipatory. "I'm sorry, Sir."

"It's a very nice apology, Becca," he mused, a hint of humor in his otherwise stern tone. "But the fact remains, you were late. And I was kept waiting. And I believe there's something missing from your wardrobe."

She lifted her head, blinking innocently. "Missing, Sir?"

His lips twitched once before settling once again into a disapproving line. "Nick?"

"You had stockings on when you left for work this morning, Rebecca," Nick said from behind her, and she turned to see him sitting the sofa next to her. "Where are they now?"

In the bottom of my office trash can, she thought, but she didn't say it. The details didn't matter—even if she'd been accosted on the street by a gang of stocking thieves, the bottom line was her stockings were gone, and she was getting whatever punishment they decided to give her. Pleading her case was part of the game, though, so she said plaintively, "They got ruined, Daddy. I had to throw them away."

"You threw them away," he repeated, in full Stern Daddy mode. "I bought you those stockings, Rebecca, especially for tonight. Is this how you treat a gift from me?"

She lowered her eyes to the floor once more so they wouldn't see the laughter. He'd bought the cheapest stockings she'd been willing to wear, knowing full well they'd be destroyed by the end of the night. "No, Daddy," she said meekly. "I'm sorry."

"Not good enough," he replied. "You owe Cade more than an apology. He's going to spank you as punishment, and you'll thank him after. Is that clear?"

"Yes, Daddy," she said softly, and turned back to Cade with what she hoped was an appropriately contrite and fearful expression. "I'm ready to take my punishment, Sir."

Cade's eyes flared, wild and hot, all his edges on full display. "Stand up."

She pushed to her feet, wobbling on the skyscraper heels that had been part of her prescribed outfit for the day, hot pink to match her lingerie. Cade shifted in his seat, sliding forward so he sat on the edge of the dainty chair. She got momentarily distracted by his shoulders, fascinated and aroused by the way his muscles bunched and moved under the thin cotton of his T-shirt. If she hadn't already been turned on by the prospect of the spanking, watching all that muscle move would've done it.

Then he patted his knee and said, "Over," in a harsh voice and she blinked back to the moment.

"Yes, Sir," she said, trying to sound appropriately chastened, and stepped forward to lie across his lap.

It was tricky and awkward, because the carved wooden arm of the chair was partly in the way and her skirt was very snug, but with a little maneuvering she managed to drape herself over his lap, butt in the air.

He was hard under her, his thighs like granite against her belly. He shifted, muscles flexing as he adjusted his position, and the firm, thick curve of his cock pressed against her hip. She put her hands flat on the floor in front of her for balance, her hair hanging in her face, and tried her best not to rub against it.

It was hard because she was really fucking horny, but she tried.

"Very nice," he said approvingly. His hand skimmed her ass, the skirt stretched tautly over it. "This is in the way, though, isn't it?"

She opened her mouth to answer him—it seemed like the polite thing to do—but all that came out was a shocked squeak when he gripped the hem of the skirt and yanked, ripping it right up the back seam so her ass was exposed.

At this rate, she wasn't going to have any work clothes left.

Cool air rushed over her bare skin and hot blood rushed to her face. "Well, well," Cade drawled. "No panties. That's very slutty of you, Becca."

Your buddy Nick wouldn't let me wear any, she would've said if she'd been able to speak, but the lust fogging her brain had rendered her mute.

"She always run around without underwear?" Cade was saying, and though she couldn't see him through the curtain of her hair, Rebecca turned her head toward Nick.

"All the time," Nick said, richly amused. "But this time, I'm afraid it's my fault. I didn't let her wear any this morning. She had a garter belt, though. I imagine it ended up wherever the stockings did."

"Hmmm." Cade ran his hand up the back of her thigh, and she arched into the caress. "Garters would look good framing this ass."

"They did," Nick confirmed.

"Too bad I don't get to see it." He tapped a finger on her hip. "I think that deserves a few extra spanks, don't you, Becca?"

"Yes, Sir," she said, and wiggled her butt.

Nick's low laugh slid over her like a caress. "I think she's ready to play, Cade."

"Is that right, Becca?" Cade shifted under her, leaning forward so when he spoke again, low and rough, his breath brushed over the back of her neck. "You ready to play?"

"Yes, Sir." Her pussy was already wet, just below his hand. She'd been wet the moment she'd sunk to her knees.

"Too bad," Cade said softly, chuckling when she jerked in surprise. "This spanking isn't for you."

She tried to turn to look at his face, but his hands held her firmly in place. "Oh, I'll warm you up," he promised in that dark, honeyed voice. "And I have no doubt you'll be just as ready to fuck when I'm done as you are now, if not more so. But I'm spanking you because it pleases me, and you're going to take it for the same reason."

She squirmed, harder this time, and his fingers curled into her hip to hold her still. She turned to look for Nick, and Cade laughed.

"Daddy can't help you now, little girl," he whispered. "You can beg, cry, scream, and he won't help you."

"Nick?" she said, fear tightening her voice.

"Your safeword still works, Rebecca," Nick said, and she latched onto the words like a lifeline.

"Okay."

"Good girl," Nick said, and she clung to his approval like a lifeline.

"You will not move," Cade said, the edge in his voice even sharper than before. "You will not try to get away from me. If you're a good girl and take your punishment without complaint, it will be short. If you struggle, complain, or try to get me to stop, I'll tie you down, gag you, and start all over again. Do you understand me?"

She hung over Cade's lap, shivering with excitement and fear as she waited for his hand to fall. "Yes, Sir."

"Oh, and count," he said a split second before he hit her.

The sharp crack echoed throughout the room, nearly drowning out her sharp cry. The pain was a jolt, rocking her forward. Heat bloomed under her skin.

"One," she gasped.

"Good girl," he said, and hit her again in the same damn spot. Pain bloomed, and with it, a hot and heavy lust.

"Two."

He spanked her again and again, steady smacks with enough of a pause in between for her to count. Arousal slid through her to settle in her breasts, in her cunt, and her clit pulsed with the beat of her heart. The heat in her butt was edging toward a deep, clawing itch that always seemed to come with heavy impact play, and she squirmed under his restraining hands.

When she hit ten, he paused, his hand warm and heavy on her butt. "What do you think?" he said, and she hoped he wasn't talking to her because she didn't think she could speak.

"Ten more," Nick said.

"Ten more it is. Keep counting, Becca."

The blows resumed, sharp and heavy, pleasure and pain knotting together so completely she couldn't separate them. She continued to count, her voice growing increasingly ragged with every blow.

"You're doing well, Becca," he murmured, his voice muffled, as though she had cotton stuffed in her ears. His hand lay heavy on her burning ass, the pressure a painful comfort. "Just a few more. Can you keep going?"

She nodded, rubbing her face against his leg. The fabric of his slacks was thin enough she could feel the heat of his skin though it. "Yes, Sir."

"Are you sure?"

She nodded again and pressed closer, needing the stability of that sturdy limb. "Yes, Sir. Please, keep going."

"All right." He patted her butt gently. "Three more. Keep count."

Her ears were ringing by the time he stopped. "You took that so well," he crooned, his hands steady and sure as he helped her to her feet. He stood with her, and her eyes were nearly level with his in her heels. He cupped her chin, urging her gaze up. His eyes were warm now, approval and affection making them soft. "Such a good girl for me. Now, I think you have something to say."

Oh, right. "Thank you for my punishment."

One dark eyebrow shot up, his eyes going hard, he tightened his grip on her chin. "Thank you, what?"

Whoops. She swallowed. "Thank you, Sir."

"Very good." His eyes softened again. "You're going to be a good girl for us tonight, aren't you?"

"Yes, Sir," she managed, then jolted with a gasp when a hand slid around her belly from behind.

"I'm proud of you, Rebecca," Nick said, his mouth so close to her ear she could feel the soft puff of his breath. She leaned back against him, seeking the familiar contours of his body.

"Thank you, Daddy." Her eyes slid closed on a soft sigh, then flew back open at the sound of Cade's low chuckle.

"Don't go to sleep, Becca," he said, his lips curled in amusement. "We're not done with you yet."

Rebecca jerked in Nick's arms, the muscles in her belly spasming under his hand. The unsteady rasp of her breathing told him she was already aroused, already on edge. They could probably fuck her right now and she'd come screaming, but it wasn't enough. He wanted her mindless with the need for release, so they still had work to do.

This was her chance to live out her fantasy, and he wanted her to have a night she'd never forget.

He swept her hair away from her neck. Her smooth skin was flushed with arousal, and her pulse fluttered madly under her jaw. It was irresistible, that soft curve, and he bent his head to drag his beard over it. It roughened with goosebumps, making him smile.

"Daddy's girl," he murmured, lips pressed against that pounding pulse. "Aren't you?"

"Yes." Her head tilted to the side in an unmistakable invitation, and he rewarded her with a scrape of his teeth.

"Are you going to be a good girl for Daddy?"

The flush on her neck deepened. "Yes," she said, her voice quivering with lust and nerves.

"Are you going to do whatever Daddy wants?"

"Yes."

He could see over her shoulder now, the way the blouse gaped open to reveal the pink lace demi bra he'd laid out for her that morning. She'd rolled her eyes and complained that her boobs were going to spill out of it and how was she supposed to concentrate with the lace scratching her all day long? But she'd pulled on the bra, and the matching garters, with a blush on her cheeks and a twinkle in her eyes, not nearly as annoyed as she pretended to be.

She sucked in a breath, then let it out in a rush when he slid his hand up from her belly, skimming over quivering breasts, to close around her throat.

He kept his grip light, and let his arm lay heavy against her chest. Neither of them considered actual choking to be a safe activity, but the implied threat of a hand on her throat was a delicious mindfuck.

"I love you, my good girl," he said softly in her ear, thrilling at the way her throat bobbed under his constraining hand.

"I love you, too, Daddy," she whispered.

He kissed the curve of her jaw, lingering there a moment, then used the pressure of his hand on her throat to urge her head back. Her hair fell away, baring flushed cheeks and dazed eyes. He tightened his hand minutely, just enough to turn her head toward Cade. "You have two Doms to please tonight. And you *will* please us. Won't you?"

Her throat worked as she tried to speak, flexing against his palm. "Yes."

His eyes met Cade's over Rebecca's head, and he gave a subtle nod.

Cade's eyes flickered in acknowledgment, then lowered to Rebecca's. "What are your safewords, Becca?"

She swallowed again. "'Yellow' for slow down or pause to talk, 'red' for stop."

"Good." Cade stepped forward so he pressed against her, sandwiching her between them. "Do you have any questions for me before we begin?"

Her head moved in a side-to-side shake so slight that Nick might not have known she'd done it if his hand hadn't been on her throat. "No, Sir."

"Excellent." Cade held Rebecca's gaze for another heartbeat, then lifted his head to look at Nick. "I want her mouth."

"Hmmm." Nick lips traced lightly over her jaw, the curve of her cheekbone. He flicked his tongue over the delicate lobe of her ear, smiling when she shuddered. "I still need to get my punishment in. I really think that should come first."

She jerked slightly in his arms at that, a small sound of protest slipping from her lips. He chuckled in her ear. "Two Doms to please, remember?"

"She's kept me waiting long enough," Cade complained, his hands slipping to her waist.

"True," Nick mused, his fingers drumming lightly on the skin of her neck and pretended to think. That he could feel her pulse hammering under his fingertips delighted him. "How about both?"

"Blow job and punishment?" Cade pursed his lips as though he was considering the idea. "If she bites me…" he said, letting his voice trail off menacingly, and Nick barely held back a chuckle at the way she went rigid between them.

"She won't," Nick replied, and left the *or else* unsaid. "Will you, Rebecca?"

She shook her head so hard she nearly cracked her head into his jaw. "No, Daddy. No, Sir."

"Good girl." Using his grip on her throat, he turned her around and pushed her toward the open doors to the bedroom. "Let's get started."

Chapter Thirteen

Nick pulled her to a stop at the foot of the bed, and Rebecca forced herself to stand still. She still wore the ruined skirt, the torn edges skimming the backs of her thighs, and her demurely buttoned blouse. She wondered how long it would be before she was divested of both.

"She's overdressed," Cade commented, right on cue.

"Go ahead and take care of that for me, will you?" Nick said, and turned to the toy bag parked on the foot of the king-sized bed. "I need to find something."

"Happy to." Cade stepped in front of her and reached for the fastening of her skirt, his dark eyes locked on hers.

"I know you're Nick's baby girl," he said conversationally, working the trio of buttons at her hip, "but tonight, you're also my fucktoy. Isn't that right?"

She nodded. "Yes, Sir."

"Say it."

Oh, God, oh God. "I'm your fucktoy tonight, Sir."

His eyes gleamed with approval. "Good girl."

The skirt dropped to the floor with a soft whoosh of fabric, and he went to work on the buttons of her blouse. The buttons were small, forcing him to go slowly. It wouldn't have been a problem except he was holding the fabric away from her body as he worked, so close and yet not touching her at all.

She really, really wanted to be touched.

She inhaled deeply, drawing in the faint scent of peppermint that clung to his skin. The action pushed her breasts toward his hands, making him tsk as he undid the last button and stepped back.

"It's not your turn yet. Take it off, let it drop."

She stifled her impatience and did as she was told, drawing the plain, starched cotton slowly down her arms. She paused to undo the buttons on the cuffs, then let it fall, as ordered, to lay on top of the skirt.

She stood in her high heels and pink bra and tried not to give into the urge to throw herself on the bed.

"Very nice." Cade's eyes roamed over her, lingering on breasts and belly and the tuft of pubic hair on her mound.

His eyes lingered on between her legs. "I've been meaning to ask why you don't keep her bare," he called out to Nick, and reached out to flick one finger at the small patch of hair. His touch was so light she didn't even feel it, and she resisted the urge to lean into it.

"She likes it that way, and I've found it useful," Nick replied, still rummaging around in his toy bag. "I'll show you later."

"I'll look forward to that." He dropped his hand and jerked his chin. "Lose the bra."

She thought about making a striptease out of it, but the sad truth was that she'd just end up torturing herself. She flicked the front clasp open so her breasts bounced free, then shrugged the straps off her shoulders and let the bra fall to the pile of clothes at her feet.

"Love these tits," Cade said. "I've tied them up twice now, and didn't get to play."

She didn't know what to say to that, and she didn't have time to think of anything because he finally—*finally!*—put his hands on her. But not on her breasts, as she'd hoped. No, he was still in teasing mode, dancing his fingertips over her belly, swirled them down to circle her navel. He dragged them through her pubic hair, tugging hard enough for her to feel this time, then slid down to her thighs.

"Well." He lifted his wicked gaze to hers. "You're making a mess of yourself, Becca."

Her answer was to press into his skimming fingertips, eager for a firmer touch.

His low laugh sent shivers down her spine.

"Greedy girl," he chided, and delivered a quick, stinging slap to one damp inner thigh. "Behave."

Nick's laugh mingled with her strangled gasp. She looked over to find him leaning against the bedpost, a long, thin piece of wood in his hand.

Cane, she realized, and her breathing quickened.

"She always such an eager little slut?" Cade asked.

"Always." Nick pushed away from the bed post, the cane dangling idly from his fingertips as he approached. "And she likes a little pain."

"She did seem to enjoy that spanking."

"Wait till you see how she flies under the cane," Nick said bluntly, sliding his hand over her ass. She had to bite back a hiss when he squeezed, fingertips digging into tender flesh.

"Can't wait," Cade purred. "But I thought this was supposed to be punishment?"

Nick grinned. "You say potato. And anyway, she won't be able to zone out on it like she usually does. She's going to be too busy sucking your cock."

She let out a soft moan, heat filling her at the idea.

"Oh, she likes that." Nick tangled his fist in her hair and forced her head back. "Is that right, Rebecca? Would you like that?"

"Yes," she gasped, sharp prickles of pain flaring in her scalp. It danced through her, tightening her nipples and slickening her pussy with arousal. "I'd love it."

"That's my slutty baby," he murmured, and took her mouth in a brief, scorching kiss. When he lifted his head, his breathing was almost as harsh as hers. "Bend over."

The room spun around her as she bent forward, his hand in her hair guiding her down. She blinked, shocked to find Cade perched on the side of the bed—she hadn't seen him move. His shirt was untucked and unbuttoned, revealing firm muscles and tan skin that made her mouth water. Then he unfastened and unzipped his slacks, and she didn't see anything else because his cock was a fucking work of art.

Hard, and already wet at the tip, he was shorter than Nick, but thick—*really* thick. She glanced up at his face to see him smiling down at her. It wasn't a reassuring smile, but a wicked one with an edge of mean, and the pulse that had taken up residence between her legs pounded a little harder.

Nick urged her forward and she stumbled a little, awkward in the high heels. When she was close enough, she planed her hands on the mattress on either side of him, grateful to be able to steady herself.

"I fucking love this ass," Nick growled behind her. The force of his hand hitting her butt jerked her forward, and she bumped her chin into Cade's bobbing cock.

"Oh, yeah, this is going to be fun." Cade wrapped one around the base of his cock and the other around the back of her head. "Put your hands on my thighs, Becca."

The thick muscles of his legs were warm under her hands, the thin slacks a soft contrast to the hardness beneath. And speaking of hard…

She swallowed, her eyes locked on his cock. It was mouthwatering, the thick vein running up the side, the flared and ruddy head. It was tan, she realized with a jolt, just like his chest, his arms, his hands. The thought of him sunbathing naked made her inexplicably want to giggle.

"Something funny?" he drawled.

"No, Sir," she managed giddily, and saw him quirk an eyebrow out of the corner of her eye.

"Your girl is sassy," he said to Nick.

"Let's beat it out of her," Nick said with relish, and the lingering humor was swept away on a tidal wave of lust.

Cade laughed, low and wicked, and tangling a hand in her hair, forced her head up. "Two things. First, if you need to safeword, pound my leg three times."

"Yes, Sir."

"Second, this is not a blow job. I'm going to fuck your face, and you're going to let me. Got it?"

She nodded, saliva pooling in her mouth. "Yes, Sir."

"Good fucktoy," he said approvingly, and she flushed with pleasure. Then he was pushing down on the back of her head, and she opened her mouth to take him in.

He filled her mouth, salty and thick. She did her best to follow instructions, keeping her jaw loose and her tongue flat as he pulled her down. The head of his dick barely brushed the back of her throat, then he pulled her smoothly back up. He repeated the action, keeping the pace smooth and the thrusts shallow, and she found herself relaxing into the rhythm.

Until on the next up stroke, when a smack landed on her ass. It took her by surprise. She was so focused on following Cade's instructions that she'd forgotten all about Nick. She jerked forward, her forehead almost making contact with Cade's abdomen, and behind her, Nick laughed.

"Don't worry about me, love. Just keep sucking that cock like a good little slut."

Cade used his hand on her head to guide her back down. "Open wider. This time, you're going to take me all the way."

She barely had time to register the words before the next blow came, hard, on the tender skin where butt met thigh. She rocked with the force of it, Cade's cock slipping farther into her throat as he guided her head down instead of forward, and she gagged.

"That's it," he muttered, holding her down when she jerked in an instinctive attempt to relieve the pressure on her throat. His hand tightened in her hair as her throat convulsed and her eyes watered. Then he was lifting her head again, and a heartbeat later the next blow came and sent her back down.

Over and over, the pattern repeated. Nick would spank her, driving her forward onto Cade's cock, then he'd pull her up and Nick would spank her again. She realized quickly that if she wanted a breath, she had to time it in the split second after Cade pulled her off his cock, and before the next blow would land. Nick was hitting her hard, each smack jolting through her like lightning. Her breasts swung under her, the nipples hard and aching for attention. She wanted to play with them, but she was afraid if she lifted her hands from Cade's thighs, she'd lose her balance.

Cade was pounding his cock into her throat now, both of his hands gripping her head, holding her steady for the skull fucking. She was making gurgling noises every time he drove deep, saliva dripping off her chin and onto his pants. Her eyes were streaming, no doubt leaving her mascara streaked down her cheeks. Her throat was sore, her butt was on fire, and she knew sitting down tomorrow would be an exercise in masochism.

She loved every second of it.

"How's her ass look, Nick?" Cade asked, dragging her down once again.

"It's fucking glowing," Nick growled, and landed another blow.

"Nice."

"Almost ready for the cane." There was a pause, the air stirring a little as Nick moved around behind her, then, "Pull her off for a second."

Cade pulled her head up and she gasped for air, staring at his satisfied face through streaming eyes.

"You're a mess." He swiped his fingers across her cheek, wet with tears and spit. He held them up for her to see, black with makeup. "A dirty, filthy mess."

She managed a shaky smile, and he laughed. "You like that, don't you?"

"Yes," she rasped, her throat raw from the forceful application of his cock.

"Me too." He leaned down and kissed her, surprisingly gentle on her already bruised and swollen lips.

When he lifted his head, he used his grip on her hand to turn her head to the side, where Nick crouched waiting.

He, too, swiped through the spit and tears on her face, his pale eyes alight with tenderness and lust. The combination never failed to make her heart sigh.

"I love you," she rasped, unable to keep the words inside.

His eyes went brilliant with joy. "My beautiful girl," he murmured, his fingertips lingering on her swollen mouth. "You're going to take five strokes of the cane for me."

"Yes, Daddy," she whispered. She could already feel herself drifting, floating off into that soft, beautiful place where she didn't have to worry about anything but him. This wonderful, amazing man who loved her.

He leaned forward to brush a soft kiss on her mouth, then rose to his feet with a nod for Cade and stepped behind her once again.

She turned to see Cade watching her with a wistful sort of sadness in his eyes. Then he blinked, and it was gone.

"Watch those teeth, now," he said. He took up fistfuls of her hair again, and nodded over her head to Nick and dragged her back down on his cock.

She sucked in a deep breath, relaxing her jaw again. She gagged as he slipped into her throat for a brief moment, exhaling in relief when her head was yanked back up. He was almost completely out of her mouth when the cane landed, and the pain hit.

Fire blasted through her already tender butt, and fresh tears sprang to her eyes.

"One," Nick said, and his words echoed in her mind. *"You'll take five strokes with the cane for me."*

She didn't have time to catch her breath this time before Cade pulled her head down again, fucking into her throat and dragging her clear before the cane fell again. She was braced for it this time, for the sting and the burn and the glorious, wonderful pain.

"Two," Nick said, and Cade dragged her head down again.

Three more times they did it, Cade fucking her throat, the need to time her breathing a welcome distraction, then Nick laying the cane across her ass and thighs. By the time she heard Nick call "Five," the tears were free-flowing once again, the pain swirling through her almost sweetly, fogging her mind as her blood pounded.

Cade pulled her up again, his hands stroking her face, her shoulders. "Such a good girl, you did so well," he crooned. "Didn't she, Nick?"

Her foggy mind registered the stroke of Nick's hands up her back, down her hips and the outside of her thighs. "So well," he agreed, his beard scratching her skin as he kissed her shoulder. "So proud of my girl."

The words were a soothing balm, bringing with them a quiet glow of pleasure. Her breathing slowed and the pain receded, not really going away but fading into the background, allowing other needs to make themselves known. Like the pounding pulse in her achingly empty pussy.

Cade stroked her hair back from her face. "Pretty, slutty girl," he murmured. "You loved that."

It wasn't a question, but she answered anyway. "Yes."

"You're wet, aren't you?" he continued. "Getting your ass spanked, caned, while I fucked your throat made you wet."

"Yes," she rasped.

He rose from the bed, his hand on her head guiding her to stand with him. "Show me."

She spread her legs wide eagerly, and reached between her thighs to delve two fingers into her dripping pussy.

They slid through with ease, so wet she could hear the squish just under the ragged sound of her breathing. She pumped once, twice, shivering with need, then forced herself to pull back out and extend her hand to him.

"That's my girl," Nick said smugly from behind her, and Cade laughed.

"Very wet." He took her hand and pulled it to his mouth, sucking her fingers in and licking them clean. Rebecca's belly clenched, her thighs quivering as he licked and sucked, making sure no trace of the fluid she'd gathered was left before pulling them out with a pop. "Just as tasty as I remember."

The memory of him licking her own juices off her mouth on St. Patrick's Day flickered through her mind, and she shuddered.

He smiled as though he knew exactly what she was thinking, then looked over her head at Nick. "What do you think? Has she been a good enough girl to get a reward?"

Nick turned her around so she faced him, and his smile made her shudder again. "A reward like your dick?"

"Oh, God," she said before she could stop herself, and both men laughed.

"Is that what you want, baby girl?" Nick asked. He kissed her, his mouth soft and sweet, a direct contrast to his words. "You want Daddy to give you a nice big cock to fuck?"

She leaned into the kiss, seeking deeper contact. "Yes, please."

"That's my greedy girl." He kissed again, hard this time, his lips lingering, then turned her around again. She blinked at Cade, standing at the foot of the bed—when had he moved?—with a bundle of green rope in his hands. "She's all yours."

Chapter Fourteen

The startled confusion in her wide gray eyes was pure fucking delight. "Daddy?"

"He's our guest, Rebecca," Nick replied, forcing a note of reproach in his voice. "Be a good girl and let him fuck your holes."

"I've already had her mouth," Cade said, running his hand down the length of rope he held. "Gonna have all three before I'm done with her."

Nick forced himself to move to the armchair under the window and sit. It was about ten feet away from the bed, the hotel's idea of a 'bedroom sitting area'. It put him close enough to see what was going on, and yet and far enough away to make it clear that right now, Cade was in charge.

"Becca," Cade snapped out, and her head jerked around.

"Sir?"

"You're playing with me now," he told her, stepping forward so his cock, which he hadn't bothered to tuck away, brushed against her belly. Nick found the way her abdominal muscles rippled at the contact almost unbearably arousing. "Tell me what your safewords are."

She pulled in a breath and let it out slowly. "'Red' for stop, 'yellow' for slow down."

"Good girl," Cade praised, and Rebecca's shoulders relaxed a fraction. "Do you need to use them?"

She shook her head. "No, Sir."

His face went hard. "Then get on the bed."

She darted one quick look at Nick, then settled onto the edge of the mattress with a wince. Nick imagined her ass was fairly sore, given the two barehanded spankings and five lashes with the cane—though he'd deliberately gone light with those, so she'd have enough energy for the rest of what they had planned.

"Lie back," Cade said, his voice brusque and impersonal, and Rebecca eased back.

"Kick off your shoes and put your feet on the bed, as close to your butt as possible," Cade continued, shaking out the bundle of rope in his hands as she complied. He took his time wrapping ropes around her legs, lashing her thighs to her calves so she couldn't straighten her legs. It was quiet as he worked, the only sounds in the room Rebecca's increasingly ragged breathing and the slithering of the rope dragging across her skin.

When he was finished, he stepped back, reaching for another length of rope from the bag, and the angle of his chair gave Nick a delightful view of his beloved, tied up and spread wide for another man.

He must have made some noise, or perhaps she was just feeling uncertain or needy, because she turned her head to look at him. Her was hair a wild tangle on the sheet, and her face was still an absolute mess. Her makeup was ruined, circling her eyes and streaked down her face. Her chin and neck were shiny with spit from the throat fucking, her mouth bruised from Cade's cock.

She was stunning, but it was her eyes that nearly brought him to his knees. They were glowing with pleasure and lust and a hint of fragile vulnerability that made him want to protect her with his life and fall on her like a rabid dog, all at the same time.

She was looking right at him, everything in her eyes for *him,* and it took all his willpower to stay where he was.

"She looks good like that, Cade," Nick commented, holding her gaze. It was one of the things he and Cade had discussed, emphasizing her status as fucktoy by talking to each other instead of to her. Judging by the flush on her chest and the way she was clenching her hands, it was just as hot for her as it was for him.

"She looks like a fucking slut," Cade replied, and her flush deepened. "Her pussy's so wet it's dripping on the bed."

"That's my girl," Nick said, and forced himself to stay in his seat instead of getting up to see for himself.

Cade turned back to the bed, more rope in his hands. "Hands up over your head."

Rebecca kept her gaze on Nick as she complied. Cade moved to wrap another length of green rope around her wrists, stretching her arms up toward the headboard. He looped the rope around the corner post, rendering her hands useless and making her breasts bounce as he tugged to test the tie. "That ought to do it," he decided, and began stripping.

Rebecca's eyes flew to Cade, and Nick took advantage of her distraction to study her.

The way her legs were tied would've allowed her to bring them together, though it didn't seem as though the possibility had occurred to her. They were spread wide, her pussy on full display, and if he'd had any doubts regarding how she was feeling about how the evening was unfolding, her wet pink cunt put them to rest.

He took a moment to enjoy the view before he shifted to eye her uptilted backside critically. His view was limited by her position, but he could see bruises from the cane already blooming under the bright red streaks. The backs of her thighs were bright pink, and the blood brought to the surface by the beating would make the skin hot to the touch.

His palms itched to feel it.

He glanced at Cade, nearly naked now, and taking his cue, rose from the chair and reached for the bag at the foot of the bed.

He managed to retrieve what he wanted before she noticed him standing there.

"Knees back," he ordered, and waited while she struggled to comply. She wiggled, wincing as the sheets scraped against her tenderized ass. He waited until she'd brought her knees as close to her chest as she could, her thighs were spread wide. Her pretty pussy was visible between them, pink and soft and slick. And just below, nestled between her round, bruised cheeks, was her equally pretty asshole.

He dropped the lube and plug he'd taken from the bag onto the mattress, then reached out and slid a finger into her pussy. She was hot and snug around him, and wet enough that he slipped right in. She moaned and tried to arch into his touch, and he slapped the outside of her thigh. "Stay still."

He pulled free then dipped back in, her inner walls rippling around him. He knew exactly how that felt on his tongue, on his cock and told himself to be patient. He tugged his finger free once more, noted that it was thoroughly coated with her arousal, and tapped on her asshole. The muscle clenched slightly in response.

"I do love this greedy little hole," he said mildly, and tapped it again just to watch it flutter before picking up the lube.

He popped the cap and squirted some onto his finger, then pressed it to her asshole. He ignored her instinctive flinch at the cool gel, making sure to work the lube in deep, then added more.

When she was taking two fingers with ease, her asshole warm and snug but no longer clamping down in reaction, he pulled them out and lubed up the plug. "You know we're both going to fuck you tonight, right?"

"I…" The words ended in a gasp when he set the tip of the plug against her and pushed. "Oh, fuck."

He just laughed. "Surprise." He pulled back slightly, added a bit more lube, and pressed forward again. "I got something new for tonight. A little bigger than you're used to, but you can take it."

Her reaction was a low, guttural grunt, her hands clenching.

"I don't know if you were paying attention," he continued mildly, working the plug in slowly, "but he's thicker than I am. I figured you could use a little more prep before he jams into your ass."

Her asshole flexed on the plug, whether from the words or the unexpected girth, he wasn't sure.

"Don't loosen her up too much," Cade protested, and Nick looked up to see him rolling on a condom. "I want a tight fuck."

"Don't worry." Nick continued to press and retreat, press and retreat, going a little further each time until he'd reached the widest point of the plug. "While you're fucking her ass, I'll be in her cunt. And in the meantime, this plug will make her cunt tight as a fist."

The plug was almost in, her asshole stretching around the widest part. He held it there for a moment, drawing it out, then nudged it forward the fraction of an inch that would take it home.

It settled into place, the flared base moving fractionally as her muscles tried to both eject it and pull it in closer. Her little grunt made him grin. "There you go," he said cheerfully, and gave her bruised ass a firm pat. "One tight cunt, as promised."

Cade stepped up to the bed. "Fuck, that's a wet, greedy hole."

Nick's gaze flicked down to her swollen cunt, redder and wetter now, and spread wide open. "Yeah, it is. Enjoy."

He gave Rebecca one hard look as he stepped back. "Give him what he wants, baby girl. Make Daddy proud."

Cade chuckled, climbing on the bed to kneel between her spread open thighs. "Yeah, Becca. Make Daddy proud," he echoed, and Rebecca looked up at him with wide eyes as Nick settled in to enjoy the show.

Cade put his hands on Rebecca's knees, pushing them further back and opening her wider so she was practically bent in half. His eyes were locked between them, hunger stamped on his face. "There's that sweet candy pussy I remember."

"You barely got a taste last time," Nick reminded him, following the script they'd laid out that day in his office.

"I know," Cade replied. "I had blue balls for days after that."

"Well, you've got time now." Nick flicked his gaze to Rebecca's face, noted her wide eyes and flushed cheeks. "Help yourself."

Cade leaned in, dragging his tongue up her thigh. She shivered, her teeth sinking into her lower lip. "Is she allowed to come?"

"Your scene, your call," Nick said with a shrug, as though it didn't matter to him one way or the other.

"Hmmm." Cade nuzzled the crease between pussy and thigh, and Nick could see the gleam in his eye from across the room. "You hear that, Becca? Your Daddy just gave you to me."

It wasn't news—they'd all heard Nick tell her to give Cade whatever he wanted—but still, she jerked in reaction.

"So here's how this is going to go," Cade continued, pushing her thighs even farther apart. "I'm going to eat this candy pussy until I've had enough. Come or don't, I don't particularly care. But you'll hold the fuck still and you'll keep the fuck quiet until I'm done. You hear me?"

She nodded, her hair clinging to her damp cheeks.

He slapped her ass, one quick blow that had her choking back a cry. "Say it out loud, little fucktoy."

"I hear you, Sir," she replied immediately.

"Good. Now shut up."

Cade stretched out on his stomach, hands firmly on her inner thighs to keep them apart, and dove face first into her pussy.

Her head fell back on a short squeak, her teeth clamped into her lower lip to hold back any further sounds, and Nick couldn't decide where to look. The sight of another man's face buried in Rebecca's cunt was exactly as big a turn-on as he'd figured it would be, and normally his eyes would be locked on the action. But he hadn't counted on her face.

He'd never watched her face when he went down on her. The logistics made it difficult, of course, and though he checked in often, he'd never been able to study her while she was getting her pussy licked.

It was fucking amazing.

The expressions crossing her face ran the gamut, from pleasure to frustration to pain and back again. She was biting her lip to keep from crying out, the cries and pleas that normally flowed from her lips trapped as she tried to follow the rules. She tugged at the ropes binding her wrists, curling and uncurling her hands into fists as pleasure built.

He could tell she was close when she began to pant, the flush on her cheeks and chest getting brighter. Her belly rippled and her muscles began to jerk, then she stiffened. Her head went back in a hard arch, her mouth falling open, and her whole body shuddered and shook as she came.

Cade didn't lift his face until she'd slumped on the mattress, limp with exhausted pleasure. Then he picked up his head and turned to grin at Nick, his face glazed in her juices.

"Candy fucking pussy," he said, his voice thick with lust, and, when Nick grinned in return, turned and dove back in.

Rebecca jerked at the contact, overly sensitive from her orgasm. There was no way Cade had missed her instinctive flinch, but he didn't appear to care. He ate her out with just as much gusto as he had the first time, pushing her ruthlessly through the discomfort and back into arousal, and when she was once again writhing on the edge of orgasm, he stopped.

Cade leered and crawled on top of her. "What's the matter, little fucktoy? You wanna come again?"

She nodded, tugging at her restraints. "Please?"

"Oh, I like that," he purred, his smile sharp as a blade. "I like begging. Do it again."

"Please, Sir," she breathed, her eyes wide and wary as he loomed over her. "Please make me come again?"

"You want to come again, you can do it on my cock," he informed her.

Nick smothered a laugh, knowing Rebecca wouldn't have any problem with that.

Cade lowered himself down so his face was only inches from hers. "Beg me to fuck you."

She licked her lips. "Please fuck me, Sir."

"You need my cock?" he asked in a whisper.

She licked her lips, her tits rising and falling with her rapid breaths. "Yes, Sir."

"Tell me."

"I need your cock, Sir," she breathed, and both men smiled at the desperate need in her voice.

He eased down so his mouth was a mere breath from hers, his hands planted on either side of her ribcage to keep him suspended above her. "And where do you need it, little fucktoy?"

"In my pussy." She writhed under him, tilting her hips up in a search for contact, for penetration. "Please, Sir, fuck my pussy."

Cade laughed softly and flicked his tongue over her lips. "What kind of pussy do you have, Becca?"

"What?"

"What kind." *Lick*. "Of pussy do you have?"

She blinked as realization hit. "A slutty pussy, Sir."

Lick. "Greedy?"

"Yes."

Lick. "Needy?"

"Yes," she moaned.

"What does it need, Becca?"

"Your cock, Sir," she said, and this time, when he licked out over her lips, she met his tongue with her own. "Please."

"Oh, you dirty, dirty thing," Cade breathed with lust-filled glee. "Nick, your girl is a nasty little slut."

"I know," Nick said, his hand on his own aching cock. He couldn't help it. "You going to fuck her?"

"Hell, yes," Cade said, and reared back on his knees.

Nick kept his eyes on Rebecca's face as Cade notched the head of his cock at her opening, watched the frustration turn to pleasure and wonder with a hint of discomfort as his friend slid into her with a smooth thrust that took him in to the hilt.

Between the fat plug and Cade's fat cock, she was being stretched to the max.

"Fuck, that's a tight hole." Cade held himself deep for a moment, hands clenched on her wide-spread legs.

"Enjoy," Nick told him, and Cade began fucking her with hard, heavy thrusts.

She lasted through barely half a dozen before she came, shuddering and crying out, her eyes rolling back in her head, and Nick had to take his hand off his dick or risk coming in his pants.

"Oh, shit, she's coming already," Cade groaned, hips pumping.

"She's got a hair trigger," Nick explained apologetically. He could imagine how her cunt was clamping down on his friend's cock, how the smooth inner muscles would ripple and pull at him. "Look at me, Rebecca."

"Yeah, look at Daddy," Cade rasped, riding her hard through her orgasm. "Show him how you look, coming on my cock."

She turned her head, eyes wide as they locked on Nick. "Daddy."

"I see you, baby," he said, forcing himself to stay put. "I see you coming on that cock."

He kept his eyes on hers as Cade rode her through the spasms, continuing to fuck her as she went limp and her eyes slid closed.

Cade pulled back, his cock glistening with her juices, and looked at Nick. "I want her ass."

"Then her ass you shall have," Nick said magnanimously, and rose from his chair.

He took a minute to adjust his cock, heavy and throbbing in his slacks, then walked toward the bed. "You get her legs, I'll get her wrists."

He reached for the rope tethering her to the bedpost, his eyes on her face. It was a radiant mess, covered in smeared makeup and dried spit. The flush had faded from her cheeks and her eyes were closed, but the faint curve of her swollen lips told him she was doing just fine.

When he lowered her arms, her eyes fluttered open, a faint wince pinching her expression before it smoothed out again.

"All right?" he asked.

"Good," she sighed, her eyes drifting closed again. "I'm good."

He chuckled and went to work on the rope around her wrists. "Don't go to sleep yet, love. We're not done."

"We are very much not done," Cade said, and Nick glanced at him. He had her legs undone and straightened out, the marks from the rope clearly visible on her skin. He'd stripped off the condom and was rolling a new one, then reached for the lube.

Nick glanced back at Rebecca. The back-to-back orgasms had taken a toll, but her shining eyes told him she wasn't done yet. "Up you come, sweetheart," he said, and pulled her off the bed as Cade climbed on it.

He held her close for a moment, savoring the feel of her in his arms, then gently turned her so she could see Cade sprawled in the center of the bed, lazily lubing up his cock.

"Look at him, Rebecca," Nick said in her ear, drawing her arms gently behind her, wrapping them in rope once again. "Look at his cock. You know why he's lubing it up?"

She shivered. "Because he's going in my ass?"

"That's right, baby." Nick tied off the rope and studied it carefully. His work lacked the elegance of Cade's, but it did the job. "Bend over."

She leaned forward to rest her face on the mattress, her bound wrists resting on the small of her back. He took a moment to assess her butt, running one rough finger down one of the cane marks. Definitely starting to bruise, and judging by the way she flinched at the contact, very tender.

He gave her a light slap just for the pleasure of watching her jump. "Reach down and open up that ass, sweetheart."

Her hands curved gracefully over her reddened cheeks, tugging them apart to reveal the base of the plug. He grabbed it and pulled, going slowly to draw it out. Her whimper, muffled by the sheet, had him gritting his teeth. He wasn't going to be able to remain a passive participant for very much longer.

He tugged the plug free and tossed it aside, his eyes riveted on the way her asshole fluttered and pulsed, gaping slightly open.

He waited until it had fluttered almost all the way closed, then laid a last smack on her ass. "Go get that cock, baby."

Rebecca reminded herself to breathe as she crawled up onto the bed. With her hands behind her back, she had to balance carefully, moving slowly as the mattress shifted under her. When her knees bumped up against Cade's legs, she lifted her gaze to his face.

He was leaning up against the headboard smiling at her, but it wasn't a nice smile. It was a Dom smile, the kind that struck fear in her heart and made her pussy wet. *Well, wetter.*

His smile spread and he wrapped a hand around the base of his cock. "Get your ass up here."

Her gaze dropped to his cock, thick and hard and glistening with lube, her stomach tightening as she imagined taking it into her ass. It would hurt, even with the preparation of the plug, and with her hands tied, she would have no way to ease herself into it.

"Oh, God."

Nick laughed. "I think she figured it out."

"Not going to help her," Cade said, equally amused. He grabbed her by the waist and pulled her closer, turning her so she faced his feet. "Straddle me."

She obeyed the best she could, stretching a leg over his lap. When her knees were on either side of his legs, he pushed her forward slightly. "Nick, give her a hand?"

"Happy to," Nick said, and, with strong hands, lifted her up.

With her hands cuffed behind her, she was grateful for his help. He picked her up as though she were a doll, holding her over Cade. "Plant your feet on the bed," he instructed, and she obeyed, leaning into him when the mattress bounced a little.

"Now," he said, his eyes gleaming the way they did when he was about to do something delightfully dirty. "Sit down."

Using the muscles in her legs, and relying on him to hold most of her weight, she began to lower herself down. Callused fingertips brushed against her backside as Cade nudged her over a fraction, then two sets of hands were bringing her down.

The first touch of Cade's slick, latex-covered cock against her asshole made her freeze.

"Big, isn't he?" Nick said conversationally with a wicked grin.

"Huge," she gasped. Oh God, it felt like there was a Volkswagen trying to make its way into her ass.

"And her asshole is tiny," Cade put in. "If I didn't know better, I'd say there's no way my cock is going to fit."

"Oh, it'll fit," Nick drawled, his eyes bright and wicked on Rebecca's as he pushed her down another fraction of an inch. Her breath caught at the increasing pressure on her anus, real pain threatening. "We'll make it fit. Lower, Rebecca."

She swallowed hard and slid down a little more. Thanks to the plug and the generous hand Cade had used with the lube, the broad head of his cock slid inside her with just a little extra pressure, and the room echoed with their twin groans.

"Fuck, that's tight," Cade muttered at the same time as Rebecca whimpered, "So big," and Nick rumbled out a laugh.

"Got a ways to go yet, babe," he said with a soft tsk. "Better get moving."

"Oh, God." She swallowed hard, her legs shaking as she tried to inch herself down.

"She doesn't get her ass moving, I'm letting gravity take over," Cade growled out, his hands tight on her hips.

"You heard him," Nick said softly, and leaned forward so his lips brushed hers. "Get that fat cock into your ass. Then I'm going to put mine in your cunt, and we're both going to fuck you."

"Okay," she managed, and his laugh puffed against her lips.

"Deep breath, now."

She had half a second to comply, then he was pushing her down, slowly but inexorably, not stopping to let her adjust. Cade's cock spread her wide, the tender skin of her anus burning and stretching. It fluttered and spasmed as her body tried to acclimate, and every time it did, there was an answering pulse in her cunt.

God, it hurt and burned and the pressure was *immense,* and it was so freaking hot she could barely breathe. She flexed her hands, useless in their bonds, and kept her eyes on Nick's face, his eyes glittering with love and lust and pride as he pushed her down, helping his friend fuck her, until she was sitting on him, penetrated fully.

"Fuck, that's good ass," Cade groaned when she finally came to rest on top of him.

Nick gripped her chin in hard fingers, forcing her gaze to his. "You like that cock?"

"Yes, Daddy."

"That's my slutty girl." He laid his hand low on her belly so his fingers just teased the edges of her pubic hair, and looked over her shoulder at Cade. "How are you doing, pal?"

"Her ass is tight," Cade grunted.

"I can make it tighter. Remember I told you this could be useful?" Nick slid his fingers into the patch of pubic hair on her mound and gave it a quick, hard tug. She gasped at the sensation, her ass tightening on his cock, and Cade groaned.

"Damn, that's hot." His hips flexed up, and his hands tightened painfully on her hips. "Do it again, Nick."

Rebecca whined as he did, the short, sharp pain making her cunt and ass tighten up. Nick laughed, tugging hard again.

"That is fun," Cade decided. "But why do you get to dish out all the pain? I'm feeling superfluous, here."

"You got two hands, don't you?" Nick asked with a wicked grin. "And she's got two tits with very sensitive nipples."

"Excellent idea," Cade purred, and wrapped his hands around them from behind. Rebecca moaned, knowing it would do no good to protest. He sat up straighter, his chest pressing into her back. She'd have been grateful for the extra support if she hadn't been worried about what exactly his plans for her breasts were.

He wrapped his fingers around her nipples, stroking gently at first. It felt so unexpectedly sweet that she relaxed, and as soon as she did, he pinched them. She arched into his touch, instinctively trying to ease the pressure. He twisted and pulled, working them hard, their pale color quickly darkening to a ruddy red.

"Cade loves torturing tits," Nick commented idly, his eyes locked on her breasts as he tugged hard on her pubic hair again.

"I really do," Cade rumbled, his low laugh vibrating through her, pinching hard. "And these are particularly sweet."

Her body was so full of sensation it was hard to know where to focus. The fullness in her ass took all her attention until Cade squeezed her nipples again, making them pulse with pain. Then Nick's fingers tightened in her pubic hair, and her attention scattered again. But the empty, needy feeling in her cunt never faded.

She wanted it filled, to finally make the fantasy a reality, but she was already so full she honestly didn't know if she could take it.

"I love watching you like this," Nick said, and she blinked up at him even as the words sent a flood of heat rushing through her. Her ass clamped down on Cade, making him grunt, and the spasm of pain sent off an answering ripple in her cunt.

Nick slid his hand out of her pubic hair and wrapped it around his cock. "Look at yourself," he said, and she looked down.

Her feet were still on the outside of Cade's thighs, bent at the knee, her legs wide open. Even in her half reclining position she could see her pussy, the lips engorged, her clit a bright pink button.

"You look good getting fucked."

"She feels good, too," Cade put in, squeezing his hands hard on her tits. It set off the same chain reaction, and this time Cade groaned.

"Every time I do this," he said, and squeezed her breasts again, "her ass ripples on my dick."

"Feels good, doesn't it?"

"It's fucking fantastic." Cade flexed his hips, driving his cock impossibly deeper.

"Oh, God," she wailed, her fingers digging into Cade's abdomen.

"Wait till you feel her come like that," Nick was saying when her ears stopped ringing.

Cade flexed again. "You going to join us?"

"In a minute," Nick assured him, still stroking his cock. "I want to watch you fuck her first."

"I can do that." Using his grip on her breasts, Cade pulled Rebecca with him as he leaned back against the headboard. She whimpered as his cock shifted inside her, and struggled not to tense up.

He dropped his hands to her wide-spread legs and reached under her, gripping her thighs just behind the knee, and lifted them so her feet dangled in the air. He pulled her up, his dick sliding almost halfway out of her ass. There was almost no friction—*thank you, silicone lube*—but her asshole burned at the stretch, and the pressure was enormous.

"Your daddy wants to see you get used, little fucktoy," Cade growled in her ear.

She lifted her eyes to see Nick staring down at them as he stroked his cock, his cheeks flushed and his eyes wild. "I want to see you use her up."

"Let's give him a show," Cade said, and began to pump his dick into her from below.

She arched when he tunneled back into her ass, a half scream ripping from her throat. He pressed into her, his groin flush with her ass, digging deep, and she writhed so hard she nearly slipped off his chest. He paused to drape her knees over his, keeping her spread wide, and wrapped his arms back around her torso. Then he dragged himself free again.

He pumped into her with long, steady strokes, not hammering but not going slow, either. With her legs wide and her cuffed hands pinned between them she had no way to limit the power or the depths of his thrusts, and he took full advantage.

"You like that, baby girl?" Nick asked, his voice little more than a guttural rasp. He'd donned a condom and was stroking his cock, the firm length of him glistening with lube in the low light. "You like getting fucked in the ass while Daddy watches?"

"I feel so dirty," she moaned, and saw the answering flare in his eyes.

"Because you are," he purred. "Daddy's dirty little fucktoy, letting his friend fuck you in the ass. You begged for it, didn't you? Begged Daddy for this."

"Yes," she choked out. Her fingers curled into Cade's rippling abdomen, digging in as sensation and need built, layer by layer, thrust by thrust.

"You want more?"

"Yes."

"Tell me," Nick demanded.

"You," she said, gasping when Cade drove into her just a little harder, just a little faster. "I want you, Daddy."

"You want this?" Nick raised one eyebrow, his lip curling into a sneer. He stroked his cock, slow and slick. "Is this what you want?"

"Yes."

"Where? Where do you want it?"

"In my pussy, Daddy," she managed, the words punctuated by Cade's increasingly hard thrusts.

His eyes gleamed down at her in sinister delight. "Beg me to fuck you."

Cade thrust into her so hard his balls smacked into her wet, open pussy, forcing another cry from her lips. "Oh God, I want your cock inside me so badly, both your cocks. Please, Daddy, please fuck your baby girl."

She'd barely gotten the last word out when he was on her, straddling Cade's legs between her thighs, guiding his cock to her wide-open cunt.

"Take it," he grunted, and shoved deep.

She tried to scream but no sound came out. Her ass was already packed, and now with Nick in her cunt she was so full, much fuller than when they role-played this with toys. Overwhelmed, turned on, and desperate to come, she could only think of one thing to say. "Please."

"Like this?" Nick asked. He pulled out, then drove back in.

"Oh, God." She strained against Cade, no longer moving beneath her, letting Nick do all the work. She tried to move against them, tried to pump herself on their cocks. But Cade had her pinned and her hands were tied, and her desperate attempt to *do something* failed miserably. She'd never been more aware of her own helplessness, and it was so hot she nearly came on the spot. "More, please more."

Nick loomed over her, rotating his hips to grind against her. "Whose slut are you, Rebecca?"

"Yours," she panted. Pinned between two hard bodies, two hard cocks, unable to move. "I'm your slut. Your little girl. Oh, please."

He reached between them for her clit, easily accessible thanks to her spread-open position, and gave it a firm slap. She gasped, Cade's groan echoing in her ear as her cunt and asshole clamped down. Nick merely grinned in sinister delight and did it again. "Slutty, greedy girl, wanting to come again. That's what you want, right? You want to come?"

"Please," she gasped, trying to move again. Her fingers dug into Cade's abdomen, clawing fruitlessly. "Please."

"Beg us." Nick nipped at her bottom lip, and she tasted blood. "Beg us."

"Faster," she gasped. "Harder. *More.* God, I'm close."

"Don't you come until I tell you," he growled, his hips plunging faster, his cock spearing into her over and over, pushing her up and down on Cade's cock too. "Don't you come."

"Oh, no." Now that he'd told her not to, it was right there. She was right there. "Oh please, I can't."

"Yes, you can." He plunged in and out, faster and harder each time. "You come without permission and I'll let Cade beat your tits till they bleed, you hear me? Wait for it."

"Shit, shit, shit," she chanted. She'd been straining toward the orgasm, and switching gears to fight it off was taking all her concentration. "Hurry, oh please."

He shifted slightly, digging his knees into the bed. Her feet bounced off his shoulders. "Beg me," he whispered. "Keep begging me."

"Please, let me come, please, oh God." The words were barely intelligible, running together in a desperate litany. "Nick, Daddy, please. I need to come, need you to come. Please."

"You want me to come, dirty girl?" His breath was coming in harsh pants. "You want my come?"

"Yes, I want it," she cried.

He drove into her deep, impaling her on his cock and Cade's, and she almost went over the edge. "You want Cade's?"

"Yes." She was babbling, all but sobbing. "Both of you, please."

"You first," he said, and she let go.

Cade's hand came around her mouth to cut off her scream as all the tension, all the pressure inside her released in a blast of pleasure and pain and heat. Her cunt spasmed around his cock, her ass on Cade's, rippling and pulling at both of them. Nick roared, the sound loud in her ear, and he grew bigger and harder inside her, then he was jerking against her, jamming her down hard on Cade's impaling cock.

"Fuck," Cade growled underneath her, his hand tight on her mouth. "I can't hold off anymore. I have to move."

Nick eased back, taking his weight off Rebecca while his cock remained half buried in her pussy. "Go," he growled.

The aftershocks of her orgasm had barely begun to fade when Cade started pounding into her, driving his cock deep once, twice before he let out a shout and held himself deep. Rebecca's eyes widened with shock as he swelled inside her, pushing against Nick's cock in her cunt. Her choked cry was muffled by the hand still clamped on her mouth, and she came again with Nick's loving eyes on her face, all three of them locked together in bliss.

Chapter Fifteen

Nick stepped out of the bedroom, closing the door quietly behind him, and crossed the dim parlor to the wet bar. He pulled a bottle of water out of the small refrigerator and was turning to head back to the bedroom when he realized he wasn't alone. Cade sat in one of the chairs—the same spindly-legged thing he'd been sitting in when Rebecca had arrived—putting on his shoes.

"Cade?"

He glanced up, concern in his eyes. "She okay?"

"Yeah. Yeah, she's fine. Thirsty, so I came out for more water." Nick held up the bottle, then tucked it into the pocket of the hotel robe he'd donned. "What are you doing?"

Cade grunted a little and tugged on his shoe. "You two should be alone," he said, fingers moving swiftly to tie the laces.

"It's a two-bedroom suite," Nick pointed out. "I thought you were going to stay, have breakfast with us in the morning."

"I was planning on it," Cade said, his head still bent over his task. "But now I think it's better if I just head home."

Nick hesitated. He'd spent so much time thinking about how living out this fantasy would affect him and Rebecca, he realized he'd barely given a thought to how it would make Cade feel.

Shame flooded him at the thought. "I'm sorry," he began.

"For what?" Cade rose, his body relaxed, his movements easy. "I had fun, y'all had fun, Rebecca got to see me naked."

He grinned, quick and wicked, the familiar humor dancing in his eyes, and for a second, Nick almost believed him.

"Then why do you look like your cat died?" Nick asked bluntly.

Cade gave a short laugh and dragged a hand through his hair. "Trust you to say the quiet part out loud," he muttered, almost to himself, then sighed.

"If we did or said anything," Nick began.

Cade held up a hand to forestall him. "Neither of you did anything," he said, then let his hand drop. "I promise. I just…saw what I'm missing, is all." He shrugged. "Not your fault."

Nick nodded, his hands balled uselessly at his sides. "You want to talk about it?"

Cade looked for a moment like he did, like he'd open his mouth and start spilling his guts. Then he shook his head. "I'll take a rain check. I better get home and see what's up with Olivia."

"Right." Nick followed him to the door. "If she needs anything..."

Cade turned at the door. "I'll let you know."

"Nick? Cade?"

Both men turned toward the bedroom door where a sleepy-eyed Rebecca stood in her hotel robe. She rubbed a hand over her face, smearing some of the eyeliner that the makeup remover wipes had missed. "What's wrong?"

"Nothing's wrong," Cade assured her as she drifted across the room. Nick extended a hand, drawing her close to nestle into the curve of his body.

She leaned her head on Nick's chest, her sleepy eyes on Cade. Her hair had been brushed smooth, and it lay like dark silk against the bright white of his robe. "I thought you were staying."

Cade gave her a slow, wicked smile, and Nick wondered if she noticed that it didn't reach his eyes.

"Looking for another round, darlin'?" he purred.

"No," she replied, and wiggled against Nick as her cheeks flushed a delicate pink. "I think I'm going to need a while to recover from the last one," she admitted, and both men laughed. "But you don't have to go."

"I'd love to stay," he said, and Nick bit his tongue. "But Olivia texted me earlier that she needs a place to stay tonight. I need to check on her."

Rebecca straightened with a frown. "What happened?"

"She says she left Kyle," Cade began.

"Is she all right? Did he do anything? Does she need anything? What happened?"

"Right now, all I know is she's crashing at my place tonight," Cade said with a smile. His eyes met Nick's over Rebecca's head in a moment of shared amusement. "I'll tell her to call you tomorrow, all right?"

"All right." Rebecca hesitated slightly, then stepped away from Nick, crossing the short distance to stand in front of Cade. Nick couldn't see her face, but when she said, "Can I give you a hug?" the tentativeness of her voice made his gut clench.

Cade looked down at her, his eyes softening. "Of course."

She went up on her toes, wrapping her arms around his shoulders as Cade bent his knees slightly to meet her halfway. She whispered something in his ear, and Nick watched a spasm of pain cross over his friend's face. Then his eyes closed and he wrapped his arms around her in return, holding her tight for a long moment before letting her go.

Rebecca clung for a heartbeat more, staying on her toes to press a kiss to his cheek. Then she dropped to her heels and stepped back into the circle of Nick's arms.

"Drive safe," Nick said quietly, and Cade nodded.

"I will." The knob turned silently under his hand, the door swinging open to the dimly lit hallway beyond. He took a step forward, into that void.

"Cade?"

He glanced back over his shoulder at Rebecca's call.

"Thank you," she said simply.

He nodded, a muscle twitching in his jaw as his gaze flicked from Rebecca to Nick, then he was gone.

The door clicked shut and Rebecca turned to Nick, her gray eyes troubled. "He's so sad."

Nick gathered her close, rubbing his cheek against hers. "I don't think it has anything to do with us, love."

"I don't like it."

"I don't either."

"Maybe you should go after him."

"He'll be okay. He knows where to find me if he wants to talk." He tucked her into his side for the walk back to the bedroom. "What'd you say to him?"

She slipped her arm around his waist and sighed. "I just told him to tell Olivia how he feels."

Nick started to nod, then jerked to a halt at the bedroom door. "What?"

"I told him to tell Olivia how he feels," she repeated, blinking up at him owlishly. "What?"

"Cade and *Olivia?*"

"Well, yeah. You didn't know?"

"How could I know?" he asked, flabbergasted.

"Well, I knew, and you've been around a lot longer than I have." She slipped past him into the bedroom.

He stared after her, still in shock. "Yeah, but…Olivia?"

She paused by the bed to slip out of her robe. "It's easy to see when you know where to look."

Nick pulled the bottle of water out of his pocket and shucked the robe. "Damn."

"What?"

"I had no idea." He slid into bed beside her. "How long has that been going on?"

"I don't know." She took the bottle from him, one eyebrow raised in question. "He's your friend. He's never said anything?"

"No," Nick said slowly. "I mean, sometimes he talks about the one that got away, but…"

"And you never asked who that might be?"

He shrugged. "I figured if he wanted to talk about it, he would."

She eyed him curiously. "What do y'all even talk about when you get together?"

"Engines," he said soberly. "War. John Wayne. The best fuck we've ever had."

She uncapped the water and sipped, her eyes clear and steady over the rim. "That better be a lie."

He grinned. "Of course it is. We never talk about John Wayne."

She poked him in the ribs, then snuggled against him with a sigh. "Thank you for tonight."

"You're welcome." He slid a hand over her hip, turning her toward him. "Any regrets?"

"Not a single one. I loved it."

"I could tell," he teased gently, loving the way her cheeks flushed with color. "No bad moments, though? Things you wish we'd done, or wish we hadn't?"

She shook her head, her hair sliding over his skin in an intimate caress. "I can't think of anything, at least not right now. You might have to ask me again when my brain isn't foggy from multiple orgasms."

"Fair enough."

"What about you?"

"Not a one. That you trusted me enough to do this for you this is one of the best gifts I've ever been given."

Her smile was impish. "Better than the birthday pictures?"

"It's a close call, but I think tonight edges the pictures out of first place." He slid his hand from her hip, gliding up over her breasts, her throat to cup her cheek. "I loved watching you come apart."

Her flush deepened. "Thanks for putting me back together again."

"Always," he promised. He bent to kiss her, lingering over it, loving the taste, the feel of her against him.

She sighed against his mouth and turned into his body, pressing close, her breasts soft against his chest. Well, mostly soft.

He lifted his head, amused, and lowered his hand to toy with one newly hardened nipple. "Really?"

"No," she said, and the absolute horror in her voice made him laugh so hard the bed shook. She poked him in the ribs again. "I'm out of commission until morning, at least."

"Hmmm." He stroked her breast, dragging the edge of his fingernail over her nipple. It hardened further, and he raised one eyebrow. "You sure about that?"

She squirmed. "No."

He laughed again, pulling her close for a quick, hard kiss. "Thank you for letting me make your fantasy come true."

"Thanks for offering." She settled against him with a happy sigh.

"Anytime, love."

"I love you, Daddy."

He pulled her closer, wanting every inch of her pressed against him. "I love you, too, baby girl."

Want to see more from this author? Here's a taster for you to enjoy!

Sun, Sea and... Satisfaction Guaranteed

Hannah Murray

Excerpt

Clio Reed closed her eyes, drew in a deep breath, and reminded herself that she was on vacation.

The little cabin was perfect. Nestled in the woods on the edge of Lake Michigan, it was accessible only by an unmarked dirt road hidden so well that even the people who owned the cabin would have trouble finding it. The wide porch was screened to keep the bugs out, and held a pair of thickly cushioned lounge chairs which were perfect for lazy summer days. She could stretch out after a morning swim in the lake with Cecil, snuggle into the thick cushions with her e-reader after lunch, and watch the sunset over the lake with a glass of wine after dinner. Cecil would stretch out on the deck's wooden planks, snoring as he slept off a day of romping in the water. She'd sleep cozy and comfortable in the king-sized bed, and the next morning, they'd get up and do it all again.

She could take leisurely walks, play with her dog and read as many romance novels as she wanted, blissfully alone. If she concentrated hard enough, she could almost smell the lake and the rich, loamy scent of the woods.

The knock on the door made her concentration waver, but she ignored it and drew another deep breath. She imagined she could hear the sounds of the woods, the chirp of crickets and the gentle rush of the wind through the trees, the creak of the porch boards under her feet as she walked to the lounger and settled in to read—

Knock, knock, knock.

Her vision wavered, nearly disappearing at the three hard raps. She grunted, an annoyed rebuke for whoever was pounding on her door forming on her tongue. She swallowed it down, wiggled to settle more firmly into her cross-legged position, and pulled the image clear into her mind once more. There was her cabin, lovely and perfect. She was lying on the lounge chair, Cecil's furry bulk on the chaise beside her, no one around to inter—

Knock, knock, knock. "Come on, Clio. I know you're in there."

"Leave me alone," she mumbled under her breath, eyes still closed, mentally in her lakefront paradise, an e-reader in her hand and her dog at her side. "I'm on vacation."

"Mom wants everyone out on the upper deck for a family meeting. She sent a message on the family chat, so I know you got it."

No, I didn't, she thought smugly. Because her phone was tucked away in a drawer, turned off as a hedge against just such a maneuver.

"You were supposed to be there ten minutes ago. You're holding everything up."

This floating nightmare isn't even underway yet, and it's already started. Ignoring her younger brother—and the small pang of guilt—with the ease of long practice, Clio rolled her shoulders, straightened her spine, and tried to find paradise in her mind once again.

"Dammit, Clio." *Bam! Bam! Bam!* "I've got better things to do than be Mom's errand boy."

"Tell her no," she shot back, then bit her lip.

"I heard that," he crowed.

"Shit," Clio muttered and opened her eyes.

Instead of the rolling waves of Lake Michigan lapping at a sandy shore, she saw the industrial carpet, cream-colored walls, and impersonal décor that made up her stateroom on the *Duchess Dream* cruise liner.

Since it was a third of the size of a budget hotel room, *stateroom* was a stretch, but calling it a floating cell had earned her a disappointed look from her mother. Cam knocked again, then rattled the knob. "Come on, Clio. You know if I go back up there without you, she's going to come to get you herself."

"I'm coming," she called, resigned and resentful, and slid off the too-soft bed to open the door.

Her brother's handsome face wore a predictably smug smile, which went perfectly with his frat-boy-on-spring-break outfit of a Ron Jon Surf Shop T-shirt, board shorts, and flip flops. "What took you so long?"

"Ha," she replied, and walked back into the room, leaving him to follow.

"Wow," he said, looking around. "This is small."

"I know." She sat down on the tiny couch, which was really just a wide, shallow chair with two small, hard cushions. The couch was too hard, the bed was too soft—she felt like Goldilocks on the cruise from hell. "Mom says it's my fault for making my reservations at the last minute."

"She's not wrong." He wandered over to look out of the porthole over the double bed. "If you'd booked when Tara and I did, you'd probably at least have a window."

"I was hoping Mom would cave."

"What an optimist." Cam sat beside her, wincing as he settled on the hard cushion. "It won't be so bad. She's been pretty mellow, actually."

"Which is why she sent you down here to fetch me."

"Okay, so mellow is probably an exaggeration." Cam patted her knee in sympathy. "But I've got something that might help."

"A prescription for tranquilizers?" she asked hopefully.

"I'm not medicating our mother."

"I meant for me."

"I'm not medicating you either." He pulled a small velvet box out of his pocket and flipped the lid open. "I'm going to ask Tara to marry me."

"Holy crap, Cameron." She stared at the ring. "Is that Grammy Reed's ring?"

"Yeah." He turned the box so the diamond caught the light. "Dad gave it to me when I told him I was going to propose. I wanted to make sure that was all right with you."

She blinked in confusion. "You want my blessing?"

"No. I mean, I'm happy to have it, but I'm talking about the ring. You're older than me, so technically, it should go to you."

"Technically, it should go to Carter," she countered. "He's the oldest."

"Dad said he'd offered it to him when he and Gabe got engaged, but they didn't want it."

Clio looked at the ring again, its delicate gold filigree and central stone gleaming in the light. "Yeah, I don't think it would fit Gabe."

"Dad told them they could keep it for their kids, but Carter said he was fine with it going to one of us."

"Cam." She reached up to cradle his face in her hands. "I'm so happy for you."

"Thanks." He squirmed a little, delighting her. "You're not going to get mushy, are you?"

"Hell, yes," she said, and pinched his cheeks for emphasis. "It's absolutely okay with me if you give Grammy's ring to Tara. It's perfect for her."

"Yeah." He looked down at the ring again, his smile going sappy. "Yeah, it is."

"When are you going to ask her?"

He snapped the box shut and tucked it away. "Tonight, at dinner. I can't wait to see Mom's face."

Clio started to point out that it wasn't their mother's moment, then bit her tongue. If Cam and Tara didn't mind, it was none of her business. "She doesn't know you're planning to propose?"

He shook his head. "I asked Dad not to say anything. You know she can't keep a secret."

Clio snorted. "He better hope she doesn't find out about that."

"I know."

"Although if she's mad at him, she won't have time to nag me this week," she mused. "Would it make me a terrible daughter if I threw him under the bus?"

"Yes." He pushed to his feet and held out a hand. "Speaking of which, we better go."

She made a face and allowed him to pull her to her feet. "Can't you just tell them I took a sleeping pill and I'm too groggy to come out on the deck because I might lose my balance and fall into the ocean?"

"No." He dragged her to the door.

"Wait!" She tugged her hand free and ran the three steps back to the bed for her long-sleeved shirt and wide-brimmed sun hat. "Okay, I'm ready."

"You know it's ninety degrees out, right?"

"Believe me, I'd prefer fewer layers." She hated covering up the cute pink top, and could have gone without the sweat she knew would gather under the brim of the hat and soak into her hair. Shorts would've been nice, too, instead of the loose cotton pants, but at least this way, she wouldn't fry to a crisp in the Florida sun.

Being a natural redhead, with the accompanying pale-as-Casper skin, could be a real bitch. Especially when both of her brothers, her parents, and every other member of her family except for Great-Aunt Francine looked like they'd just stepped out of the pages of a surfing magazine after five minutes of sun.

"Can't you just wear sunblock? You look like somebody's grandma."

She smacked him on the arm. "I'm wearing sunblock, you ass. I still burn."

"Like a vampire," he muttered, wincing when she smacked him again. "Ow. Quit hitting me."

"Quit being a dick," she shot back and smacked him one more time for good measure. "Let's get this over with."

"Wait." He turned back at the door. "Tara asked me to get her a bottle of water. Can I have one of yours?"

"I don't have any bottles of water."

"What's that?" he said, pointing past her to the nightstand.

"That's distilled water."

"So?"

"So, it's for my CPAP."

"Your what?"

She pointed at the sleek little machine on the nightstand. "The thing that helps me breathe while I sleep?"

"Oh, right. Can't you refill it at the sink?"

"No, jackass, I can't. I have to use distilled water, or the minerals in the tap water fuck up the machine."

He frowned. "That sounds made up."

She shoved him out of the door. "You can't have the water, Cameron."

"Then I have to go back to our room to get one of ours."

She checked her pocket to make sure she still had her key card, then pulled the cabin door shut behind her. "So go. I'll meet you up there."

He narrowed his eyes, suddenly suspicious. "Give me your key."

"What? No."

"I don't trust you not to go back in there and bar the door."

She rolled her eyes as though she hadn't been considering exactly that. "Get a grip, Cameron."

She headed down the narrow hallway, Cam on her heels. "Listen, our room is on the deck above you. Why don't you come with me? You can have a bottle of water, too."

"I don't need a bottle of water, I'm very well hydrated." She bypassed the bank of elevators in favor of the wide central stairwell and began to climb. "Go, Cam. I promise I won't run away."

"Okay. Tell Mom I'll be right there."

She waved a hand and continued up the stairs as he veered off. Half a flight later, she heard footsteps behind her again and stopped climbing with an aggravated sigh.

"Cam, I said I would go," she began, turning to confront her brother, and found herself face to face with a stranger. "Oh. You're not Cam."

"No, I'm Fox," he said, and smiled. "Hello."

"Hello," she replied automatically, while her brain sounded the hot-guy alert.

Seriously hot guy. He was big, towering over her even though he stood two steps lower, and handsome. He had dark hair curling over his ears, misty green eyes, and a jaw covered in dark stubble that looked like a vacation beard in the early stages. He wore a plain black T-shirt, khaki cargo shorts and flip flops, and a smirk on a beautiful mouth that, aside from his hair, looked to be the only soft thing about him.

She blew out a breath and tried not to drool.

She didn't speak, and would've sworn that her expression didn't change even a smidge. But his smirk deepened and his eyes lit with amusement, and it made her want to kiss him and punch him at the same time. To prevent herself from doing either, she said, "What kind of a name is Fox?"

"Family name." His gaze flicked down then up again, and she fought the urge to squirm in her long pants and long sleeves and grandma hat. "It's Foxworth, but since that makes me sound like one third of a tight-ass accounting firm, I just go by Fox."

"Good call," she said, and with nothing to say besides *can I sit on your face?*, turned and began climbing the stairs again, automatically keeping tight to the rail so he could walk past her.

He didn't.

"Who's Cam?"

She paused and turned to frown at him, still two steps below her. "What?"

"Who's Cam?" he repeated. "You said, 'you're not Cam', so who's Cam?"

"My brother," she said absently, trailing her gaze down his body again. His shoulders were broad, his chest and arms thick. He had actual, visible muscles in his forearms, which were tan like the rest of him and dusted with dark hair. *Forearm porn of the highest caliber*, she thought hazily and turned to continue up the stairs, holding on to the railing so she wouldn't fall, trip him, and drag him on top of her.

"What's your name?" he asked, keeping pace behind her.

"None of your business," she replied automatically, because really, it wasn't.

"True," he said easily, her don't-fuck-with-me tone having no effect on his friendly cheer. "I only asked because it's expected. Social niceties and all. I don't really want to know."

That was just what she needed, sarcasm from a hot stranger. She sniffed and kept climbing, trying not to be annoyed because her ass looked flat in these pants.

"I don't need to know, anyway," he continued. "It's not like we're family or anything. Hell, we'll probably never see each other once we get out of this stairway."

"If there's a God," she muttered, already mourning the loss of his forearms.

"Unless we want to see each other outside of this stairway, of course."

"Why would we want that?" she blurted out without turning around.

"I don't know." He was, annoyingly, not at all out of breath from the climb. "Maybe because you think I'm hot."

She missed the next stair and stumbled, barely catching herself on the railing in time to keep from falling on her face.

"Careful there," cautioned a young man in a crew uniform coming down the stairs. He had soft brown eyes, a pretty face and what looked like a pleasingly muscled form under his crisp uniform. "You all right?"

"Yes, thanks." She smiled at him, and his smile broadened in return.

"Here, let me help you." He stepped closer, holding out a hand.

"She's fine," Fox said from behind her and hauled her up with a strong arm around her waist. "Aren't you, darling?"

"Peachy," she said through gritted teeth and resisted the urge to kick him.

"Right." The young man's smile went from warm and interested to coolly polite. "Keep hold of the railing, now."

"Thanks," she said, watching as he continued down the stairs, taking her first prospect of a shipboard hookup with him. Annoyed, she turned to glare at Fox. "Do you mind?"

"Sorry," he said, not sounding sorry at all, and pulled his arm from around her waist. "Just trying to help."

"Cockblocking me from the cute sailor is not helpful," she muttered under her breath and started climbing again.

"Sorry, what was that?"

"Nothing." She stopped on the stairs again and turned to glare at him. "What did you say?"

"I said 'sorry, what was that?'," he replied with a frown. "Did you hit your head?"

"No, I did not hit my head. Before that, when I fell. You said something."

"Oh." His frown faded and the smirk reappeared. "The part about you thinking I'm hot?"

She tried not to stare at the way his shoulders moved in the black t-shirt. Or the way his forearms flexed as he shoved his hands into his pockets. And she certainly didn't remember how it had felt around her waist, thick and hard and deliciously restraining. "I don't."

"Don't what?"

"Don't think you're hot." *Liar, liar, pants on fire.*

"You don't?"

She planted her hands on her hips and scowled. "No."

"Oh." He shrugged and smiled, unconcerned. "Sorry. My mistake."

"Don't mention it," she replied, oddly disappointed, and started up the stairs again.

"I probably shouldn't have assumed that," he continued, "just because you were staring at me."

I wasn't staring. In fact, I made a point not *to stare.*

"The fact that I checked you out doesn't mean anything either," he went on blithely as she ground her teeth together. "I mean, I did check you out, but that certainly doesn't mean I find you hot."

Clio kept silent as she reached the top landing, biting her tongue to keep quiet, and crossed to the doors leading out to the deck.

"Not that you're not attractive." He followed her out, unfortunately catching the heavy door before it slammed in his face. "You seem lovely, even in those clothes. Are you a member of some kind of religious order that prohibits shorts or something?"

She jerked to a stop and turned to him, her scowl not at all feigned this time. "Yes, actually. Sister Theresa

Grumpy Pants of the Order of Perpetual Boob Sweat. Nice to meet you. Would you like a brochure?"

He flashed a grin, quick and delighted. "Hey, you *do* have a sense of humor."

"I'm a fucking laugh riot," she muttered and kept walking, completely unsurprised when he fell into step beside her. "Is there a reason you're following me?"

"I'm not following you," he told her. "I'm meeting my family up here."

"Right."

"Seriously. Not everything is about you, Theresa. Can I call you Terry?"

She refused to smile. "Sure. Foxworth."

"Touché." He leaned forward to peer at her face, keeping pace with her easily. "Are you sure you don't think I'm hot? We could have dinner later. Maybe play a game of shuffleboard."

"Are you using 'shuffleboard' as code for some deviant sexual act?"

"Would you say yes if I was?"

She just might. He *was* hot, and charming, and she figured he owed her an orgasm or two for cockblocking her with the sexy, brown-eyed crewman. The possibility of a shipboard romance with a handsome stranger—and by romance, she meant wild sexual romp with absolutely no feelings involved—was the only thing keeping her from diving over the side of the ship and making a break for it. Well, that and the knowledge that her mother was a very strong swimmer, and would no doubt come after her.

She sent him a speculative glance, taking in his cheerful grin and handsome face. There was a slight breeze out on the deck, making his hair float up around his head like a dark halo. And his forearms were still flexing, porn-like.

He caught her eye and sent her a saucy wink. "Okay, just dinner. We'll find a secluded table for two and you can tell me all about perpetual boob sweat. Who knows? Maybe I'll join the order."

"I only have to get two more recruits to win the toaster oven." She refused, absolutely refused to laugh. "Are you always this chatty?"

"Depends on how much the other person talks," he said easily. "Though I am sometimes very, very quiet."

She gave a skeptical snort. "When?"

"When I'm sleeping, eating, or performing cunnilingus."

The laugh burst out before she could catch it, and he grinned.

"There it is," he said. "I knew you had at least one in you."

"Have you been trying to make me laugh?"

"Sure. People are always more willing to say yes to things when they're in a good mood."

"What are you trying to get me to say yes to?"

His grin was wicked. "Me."

"Of course," she said, more than tempted to say yes to dinner and cunnilingus. A tongue that got as much exercise as his did was bound to have stamina. But she could see her family ahead, her mother's blonde head next to her father's blond head, her other blond relatives nearby, and the anxiety that had been surprisingly absent since he'd said, "*No, I'm Fox,*" in the stairwell was creeping in again.

It was remarkably difficult to say, "I'm afraid I'll have to pass."

"You sure? Satisfaction guaranteed. I'll even wear a gag if you want."

She managed to choke back another laugh. "Intriguing, but yeah. I'm here with my family."

"Ah. Well, if you change your mind, I'll be around. It was nice to meet you, Sister Theresa."

"Likewise, Foxworth."

"And who knows? Maybe our paths will cross again."

They were only a few feet away from her family now. She shook her head. "I doubt it."

"Never say never," he said with a wink, just as a tall figure with bright red hair broke free from the crowd.

"Darling, *there* you are!" Aunt Franny, resplendent in a flowing orange caftan with purple flowers and gold trim, came flying toward them. She wore chandelier earrings that brushed her shoulders, blue eyeshadow, and her bright red hair—cut in the same Dorothy Hammel hairstyle she'd been wearing for as long as Clio could remember—was topped with a tiara that sparkled in the late afternoon sun.

"Aunt Franny," she began, then stood stock still, her mouth open in shock, as Franny's outstretched arms wrapped Fox in an enthusiastic hug.

"Hi, Mom," he said and winked at her over Franny's silk-covered shoulder.

Sign up for our newsletter and find out about all our romance book releases, eBook sales and promotions, sneak peeks and FREE romance books!

About the Author

Hannah has been reading romance novels since she was young enough to have to hide them from her mother. She lives in the Pacific Northwest with her husband—former Special Forces and an OR nurse who writes sci-fi fantasy and acts as In-House Expert on matters pertaining to weapons, tactics, the military, medical conditions and How Dudes Think—and their daughter, who takes after her father.

Hannah loves to hear from readers. You can find her contact information, website details and author profile page at https://www.totallybound.com

www.ingramcontent.com/pod-product-compliance
Lightning Source LLC
LaVergne TN
LVHW091046080826
845145LV00002B/640
9781839437229